"I'll be frank with you, Captain. Not many think Maximilian has a chance. But those of us he's helped owe him loyalty. So long as Maximilian rules Mexico, the old South has a chance to survive."

Slocum thought about that, and what it would mean. The language would be strange and the terrain unfamiliar and the uniforms different, and he wouldn't be fighting for something he believed in, like last time. But it would be a fight just the same... something he was starting to realize he didn't want to live without...

OTHER BOOKS BY JAKE LOGAN

RIDE, SLOCUM, RIDE
HANGING JUSTICE
SLOCUM AND THE WIDOW KATE
ACROSS THE RIO GRANDE
THE COMANCHE'S WOMAN
SLOCUM'S GOLD
BLOODY TRAIL TO TEXAS
NORTH TO DAKOTA
SLOCUM'S WOMAN
WHITE HELL
RIDE FOR REVENGE
OUTLAW BLOOD
MONTANA SHOWDOWN
SEE TEXAS AND DIE
IRON MUSTANG
SHOTGUNS FROM HELL
SLOCUM'S BLOOD
SLOCUM'S FIRE
SLOCUM'S REVENGE
SLOCUM'S HELL
SLOCUM'S GRAVE
DEAD MAN'S HAND
FIGHTING VENGEANCE
SLOCUM'S SLAUGHTER
ROUGHRIDER
SLOCUM'S RAGE
HELLFIRE
SLOCUM'S CODE
SLOCUM'S FLAG
SLOCUM'S RAID
SLOCUM'S RUN
BLAZING GUNS
SLOCUM'S GAMBLE
SLOCUM'S DEBT
SLOCUM AND THE MAD MAJOR
THE NECKTIE PARTY
THE CANYON BUNCH
SWAMP FOXES
LAW COMES TO COLD RAIN
SLOCUM'S DRIVE
JACKSON HOLE TROUBLE
SILVER CITY SHOOTOUT
SLOCUM AND THE LAW
APACHE SUNRISE
SLOCUM'S JUSTICE
NEBRASKA BURNOUT
SLOCUM AND THE CATTLE QUEEN
SLOCUM'S WOMEN
SLOCUM'S COMMAND
SLOCUM GETS EVEN
SLOCUM AND THE LOST DUTCHMAN MINE
HIGH COUNTRY HOLDUP
GUNS OF SOUTH PASS
SLOCUM AND THE HATCHET MEN
BANDIT GOLD
THE DALLAS MADAM

JAKE LOGAN
SOUTH OF THE BORDER

BERKLEY BOOKS, NEW YORK

SOUTH OF THE BORDER

A Berkley Book/published by arrangement with
the author

PRINTING HISTORY
Berkley edition / June 1984
Second printing / July 1984

All rights reserved.
Copyright © 1984 by Jake Logan.
This book may not be reproduced in whole or in part,
by mimeograph or any other means, without permission.
For information address: The Berkley Publishing Group,
200 Madison Avenue, New York, N.Y. 10016.

ISBN: 0-425-07139-1

A BERKLEY BOOK® TM 757,375
Berkley Books are published by The Berkley Publishing Group,
200 Madison Avenue, New York, N.Y. 10016.
The name "BERKLEY" and the stylized "B" with design are
trademarks belonging to Berkley Publishing Corporation.

PRINTED IN THE UNITED STATES OF AMERICA

1

Slocum jolted out of sleep so suddenly it brought him half upright in his bedroll.

For the space of a breath, he stayed propped on one braced hand, sure he'd heard the rumble of the herd stampeding again. There was no moon in the starlit sky. Off to the west he heard the faint strains of a song from one of the night guards circling the bedded steers. Then he saw the cook moving around the fire by the chuck wagon, smelled biscuits cooking, and heard the clank of a coffeepot lid, and he knew that that was what had brought him awake. Relieved, he lay back for another few minutes' rest before rolling out.

Judging by the angle of the Big Dipper, it was after four in the morning. Not too long after, because Cookie hadn't bellowed his breakfast call yet. Still, it was little more than two hours since the last time the herd had broke. A brief storm—all thunder and lightning, no rain—had spooked them at about nine the night before, and they'd been jumping and running ever since. Slocum was still groggy from lack of sleep.

Matt Snell was up on one elbow in the bedroll beside him, wiping the sleep from his eyes. "Think I'll roust out and get some of that coffee before this bunch beats me to it," Snell said.

"Believe you got the right idea," Slocum said, and reached for his boots.

He was already swabbing a biscuit in a tin plate of bacon and beans when Cookie shouted the others awake. The snoring stopped and the groaning started as men who'd had little sleep for days rolled out of their blankets. Slocum watched them pull on their boots, wet their faces at the chuck wagon's water barrel, and dry on the communal towel before coming sleepy and silent to fetch their breakfast at the fire.

Matt Snell was hunkered down beside Slocum, sipping at his coffee. "Going to be a hard day," he said.

"Won't argue with you there," Slocum said.

"At least them steers got tired of running. I ain't had a good night's sleep since this drive started. Be all I can do to stay in the saddle today."

Slocum knew the feeling. Once a herd stampeded, it seemed to develop a taste for it. This one had stampeded the first night on the trail, a month back, in early April, and had been spooking regularly ever since. His bones ached from too many hours in the saddle, his jeans were so dirty they felt greasy, and it seemed he'd never get the dust out of his eyes. And it would be two months before they reached Nebraska, where the herd was destined to become beef for the crews laying track on the U.P. Railroad building west out of Omaha. Be damned near July before they got paid out. At thirty a month, it was a hard way to make a hundred dollars.

But better than chousing mavericks out of the south Texas brush, which he'd been doing for over a year, since leaving Georgia late in Sixty-five. And he had no choice but to stick it out: he had less money in his pockets now than he'd had mustering out of Bobby Lee's army after Appomattox.

"We lose any cattle?" Snell said.

"I talked to Mr. Warren," Slocum said. "Said he figured about forty head are missing."

"He going to leave somebody to gather 'em up?"

"Don't know. Didn't ask him. Afraid he might pick me."

"Maybe them four'll drop by again. Offer to round 'em up at a dollar a head. Might have a little fun then."

"I believe you're right," Slocum said. "I don't expect even old Mr. Warren would stand for that trick a second time."

The last morning they'd come up missing steers after a stampede four hard-looking men had ridden into camp offering to round them up so the trail crew could move the herd on. Slocum figured it for a tricky bit of business—four men starting a stampede and looking to collect on their dirty work—and he hadn't liked it when Mr. Warren, the trail boss, had agreed to the deal, even for the fifty cents a head they'd settled on. As it was, they'd got only half the steers back, and even Warren agreed the others had likely got rustled off. There'd been some hot talk around the fire that night and, restless as everybody was, there might be some gunplay if the four showed up again.

Nobody liked being cheated, even out of somebody else's cattle.

Two riders had gone out to relieve the last night guards, who galloped in now to grab some breakfast. Rumbling hoofbeats approached from the other direction: the wrangler bringing the remuda in.

Snell dashed the dregs of his coffee into the fire and got to his feet. "Time to point your nose north. Another day or two and we'll cross the Red River out of Texas."

"Good," Slocum said. "I'm tired of Texas."

In the makeshift rope corral to the side of the chuck wagon he roped out his buckskin and threw the saddle on. Other men were throwing their bedrolls in the back of the wagon, and Mr. Warren was already heading out to look for a good spot to noon up. When the rest of the crew had their mounts picked out, the ropes were removed and Cookie stowed the chuck box in the back of the wagon and drove off toward the front of the herd, all his pots and pans clanging.

Slocum stuck a boot in the stirrup and swung up into the saddle. The buckskin crow-hopped in a tight circle, but it was only testing to see if he was alert; once things settled down he rode off through the cattle to take up his post on the point.

He was fully awake now, and with the hot coffee and some grub in him, getting up so early didn't seem half bad. It reminded him of the war—waking in the dark, moving out at first light toward something you couldn't see but knew could maybe be dangerous. Those memories came often to him now, especially when he rose out of sleep, and it never ceased to surprise him that the memories were good ones, that the war was something he liked to look back on, something he missed.

He always had a little of that feeling here—good men working together in dark and day, living in their clothes and sleeping on the ground, risking their necks for very little pay and very little glory. Only the scent of blood was missing, the stir of excitement that came when you knew you were going into battle. It was hard to admit that was what he missed the most.

It was near noon when he saw Matt Snell coming up through the dust alongside the strung-out herd. They'd let the cattle drift and graze a couple of miles before throwing them onto the trail, and they'd covered another five or six miles in the time since. Slocum was glad to be one of the point men today: this was a particularly dusty stretch of trail, judging by the look of Snell when he drew rein alongside the buckskin.

Snell yanked down the dusty kerchief he'd had up over his nose. "Where's Mr. Warren? He still out looking for a place to noon up?"

"If he is, we ought to be catching up with him. It's close on to noon now. What's up?"

"Four men riding up from the south. Might be them four from the last stampede. Thought Mr. Warren oughta be warned."

"There he is now," Slocum said. "Up ahead there."

They had cleared a rise of ground so slight and gradual it could hardly be seen, and far out ahead now he saw Warren making a wide circle on his bay, showing the spot he'd picked for noonday pasture. The bay came to a halt facing west, and Slocum saw the chuck wagon heading toward it.

"Looks like we're nooning here," he said. "Better get clear before we start turning these cattle. Let me know what happens. I got first shift on loose-herding."

Snell kicked his horse on past the lead steers, and Slocum dropped back a ways, letting the point man on the other side begin pushing the nose of the herd to the west, starting them in a large circle that would leave them grazing easy enough to be watched by shifts of two while the rest of the men had a quick dinner. He watched the rear of the string, but he could see nothing for the dust, and by the time the dust had settled, he was far on the other side of the herd, starting his first slow circle.

He had made one complete round when Snell caught up with him again, riding at a trot this time. "Mr. Warren sent me out to relieve you," Snell said. "You're wanted at the wagon."

"Warren wants me at the wagon? What for?"

"Not Warren. Them four men I told you about. One of 'em says it's you they want to see. Old gent, gray-bearded. Says you fought together during the War. Didn't catch his name, but he mentioned Manassas."

Slocum looked off toward the chuck wagon, but it was too far away to make anybody out. "Manassas. Which time, I wonder. Hell, that was a long time ago."

"All I heard was he was a colonel," Snell said. "You go on. I'll take over here."

Slocum turned the buckskin and started making his way back around the herd, wondering who would have trailed him all the way out here. A colonel at the Battle of Manassas. Slocum had fought at Manassas— what the bluebellies called Bull Run—both times, in

Sixty-one and Sixty-two, but even that last time had been close to five years ago, and he had no special memory of any colonel there. Nor any idea why a former Rebel colonel would be hunting him down a month up the trail toward Nebraska.

He rounded the north end of the herd and started toward the chuck wagon, where the rest of the crew was squatting around the fire. Four strange horses were tethered to the branches of a lone mesquite tree twenty yards this side of the wagon, and four men were hunkered down around the trunk, eating from Cookie's tin plates. One of them, a stocky short-legged man in a Confederate officer's tunic, put his plate down and got to his feet as the buckskin approached. When Slocum dismounted, the man removed his gray campaign hat and came out to offer his hand.

"Been a long time, Captain," he said. "I don't expect you even remember me."

Slocum remembered that reddened face and the gentle smile very well. "Colonel Lewis," he said, and shook the colonel's hand. "Been a long time for sure. Since Manassas in Sixty-two. But I don't forget faces from the war. Jim Greenleaf told me he'd seen you after Appomattox. Said you were on your way to Mexico."

"Yes," Lewis said. "Tried to get Jim to go with me, but he wouldn't. Had himself set up dealing cards in a place in New Orleans then. Come meet my friends here."

Slocum ground-reined the buckskin and loosened the saddle cinch, wondering what Lewis was after. Lewis had been one of the staunchest Confederates Slocum had ever known—and was still, judging by the Confederate garb he still wore. Colonel Robert E.

Lewis, called the General by his men, not only because his name resembled that of old Bobby Lee nor because his gray beard and short legs made him look like Lee, but because, like Lee, he had left the Union he loved to fight for the state he loved even more and in the process lost everything he'd had: a wife, two sons, and the one thing he'd loved more than any of those—his career in the army, the drill and the duty and the call to arms, the sense of belonging to a cause that lifted him above the run of ordinary men. If Lewis had followed him damned near all the way to the Red River, it wasn't just to pay a simple and nostalgic visit to an old comrade-in-arms.

Lewis was waiting under the tree, holding a plate of grub with a fork already in it. "Sit and eat," he said. "I had Hodges here fetch a plate when I saw you coming. Gentlemen, meet John Slocum. Captain John Slocum the last time we saw each other. A good man to have on your side in a battle."

Slocum shook hands with the other three as Lewis introduced them: Lieutenant Brown, a tall, boyish young man Lewis said had been his aide in the last days of the War; Corporal Hodges, younger still, who had also served with Lewis in those last days; and a weathered cowhand named Flaherty.

"The lieutenant and Corporal Hodges were with me in Mexico," Lewis said. "Mr. Flaherty agreed to guide us up here when we learned you were on this drive. You took some finding, Captain. We've about worn those horses out trying to catch you."

"You must have wanted to find me pretty bad. How'd you know where to look?"

"I looked up Jim Greenleaf in New Orleans. He said you'd signed on at the Rocking R. Jim is working the Mississippi riverboats now. Better with cards than he ought to be, they tell me, but still a good man in a fight. I'm pleased to say he's joining up with us."

Slocum watched the rest of the trail crew sneaking sidelong looks from their circle around Cookie's fire. They were as curious as he was about why Lewis had tracked him all this way. "Joining up to do what?"

Lewis eyed him over a tin cup of coffee. "You have any idea what's been going on down in Mexico?"

"No, I can't say as I have. Been sticking pretty close to the Rocking R. Why?"

"There's a war going on in Mexico, Captain. One that's threatening to destroy what's left of the old South. We don't aim to let that happen."

"Last I heard, the old South was done and gone. Buried at Appomattox. One of the reasons I left Georgia."

"Maybe done and gone for most, Captain, but not for us. You never heard of the Chivalrics, I guess. Five thousand of us emigrated to Mexico. Called ourselves the Carlota Colony. The cream of the Confederacy, in some cases. General Jubal Early. Generals Magruder and Kirby-Smith. The governors of Kansas and Missouri. We had thousands of acres and thousands more promised. Even had a ministry in the Mexican government. All because the Emperor, Maximilian, invited us to settle there. And now the rebels under Benito Juarez are close to toppling Maximilian's government."

Slocum had scraped his tin plate clean. Now he hauled a sack of Golden Grain out of his vest pocket and set about building himself a smoke. He was beginning to get an idea what Lewis was out here for. "I gather you aim to stop them," he said.

"We're aiming to help. Maximilian had the French supporting him—they put him on the throne three years ago—but they withdrew their troops in February. He could have abdicated and left them—he's Austrian, an archduke, brother to the Hapsburg Emperor—but he chose to stay and lead his Imperial army against the Juaristas. But the Imperial army's mostly ill-trained peasants. And outgunned. The United States is secretly supplying Juarez with their new Henry repeating rifles. General Sheridan smuggles them across the Texas border."

Slocum tucked the makings back in his pocket and touched a match to his cigarette. He knew what Lewis was after. He was testing the idea in his mind now, getting the feel of it, remembering how it had been, the good things and the bad. He remembered some pretty bad times, but even the bad times got all painted over in your memory.

"Colonel, I get the feeling you're out here recruiting."

"You can call it that," Lewis said. "I've spent the three months since February trying to raise a battalion to fight on the Emperor's side. Looks now like I'll be lucky to get a company together."

"What about all those ex-Rebs in your Carlota Colony? Seems like they'd have good cause to fight."

"The Juaristas overran the colony some time ago. Most everybody fled back to the States. I'll be frank with you, Captain. Not many think Maximilian has a chance. But those of us he's helped owe him loyalty. So long as Maximilian rules Mexico, the old South has a chance to survive."

Slocum was thinking about those ex-Rebs the Juaristas had driven back to the States. Sounded like Juarez's troops pretty much had the run of the country, and what little help Lewis could get together wouldn't do that Austrian archduke much good. And what was an Austrian archduke doing calling himself Emperor of Mexico, anyway?

But he found himself being pulled toward the idea just the same. The chance to fight as an independent unit, without having to answer to some vague force up the chain of command—that was the best way to fight. And a good fight cleaned a man's blood out.

"I'll tell you what I've got so far," Lewis was saying. "I've got a man in Mexico organizing and training as many locals as he can recruit. A good man, Lee Bradley. Fought as a company commander under John Bell Hood. I've got another half-dozen men scouting the Texas border. Soon as they find how Sheridan gets those repeating rifles to Juarez, we're going to steal ourselves a shipment. When we've done that, we'll smuggle them into Mexico ourselves, rendezvous with Bradley and his men, and join up with Maximilian."

"And where do I come in? Or are you just looking for another gun?"

"You're a battle-seasoned officer, and a good one. That's of value to me. And I promised Jim Greenleaf I'd look you up. Greenleaf wants you working with him."

"Doing what?"

"Getting us a boat. We have to transport that shipment of repeaters to Maximilian's troops. Best way is inland by rail from the port of Vera Cruz, and for that we need a boat that can navigate the Gulf. Greenleaf's planning to steal one out of New Orleans."

Slocum thought about that, and where it would

lead, and what it would mean. The language would be strange and the terrain unfamiliar and the uniforms different, and he wouldn't be fighting for something he believed in, like last time, but it would be a fight just the same, something he was starting to realize he didn't want to live without.

He knew he was different. Most of this trail crew had fought in the War, and from talk around the fire he knew memories still lingered with them all, memories that kept some awake hours after turning in and brought others of them shaking up out of sleep with the fear they were back in it. He seemed alone in savoring those memories like fine liquor that would bring his sluggish blood alive again, make life again worth living.

He took a last drag on his cigarette and ground it out under the toe of his boot. "Where do I tie up with Greenleaf?"

"You're with us, then. Good. Very good." Lewis set his plate down, wiped his mouth with a handkerchief, and reached across to shake Slocum's hand. "Jim will be glad to hear that. Glad as I am. He makes a run from New Orleans to Chicago and back on a paddlewheeler called the *River Queen*. Should be passing the mouth of this Red River we've been riding toward in about four days, on the downstream run. Could you get there by then?"

"Probably. I'd have to leave now and stay long hours in the saddle, but I could make it."

"Good. You can board her there. Jim says she stops there to take on fuel."

"I take it you're not going that way."

"We're heading back south. My men should have traced those rifle shipments by now. Next step is to intercept one of them. Jim can fill you in on the rest. Things work out right, we'll meet up in Corpus Christi. Sorry to say I can't offer any wages in advance, but there'll be plenty coming when this is over."

"Glad to hear it," Slocum said. "What I'll get paid off here won't be much. And Mr. Warren, our trail boss, ain't going to like me cutting out now." He got gingerly to his feet, looking off toward where Warren was watching with the rest around the chuck wagon. "As a matter of fact, you all ain't going to be too popular when Warren learns you hired me away. Maybe you ought to head on out. I'll pay your respects to the cook."

2

Four days later, Slocum caught the *River Queen* at the first woodyard below the mouth of the Red.

He had sold his horse and laid up almost a day while several other sidewheelers pulled in to take on wood, and it wasn't until after sundown that the *River Queen* hove into view, her tall twin stacks forward of the pilothouse trailing plumes of smoke. When she was tied up alongside and the black gang began loading on the cordwood she burned for fuel, Slocum carried his gear aboard and secured his passage, booking a single cabin on the portside just ahead of one of the huge covered paddlewheels that drove her. There were better cabins, but a little noise was worth the savings. Never tell how this job of the colonel's was going to turn out.

Dark had set in by the time the fuel bin was stocked and the captain called to cast off lines and the big boat thrashed off down the river. Slocum made his way forward and up the curving stairs just aft of the prow, coming out onto the boiler deck. The *River Queen* looked nearly new, with polished brightwork and gleaming rails. He made his way along the deck, past the doors of several staterooms, till he reached the Grand Saloon. If what Lewis had told him was correct, that would be where he would find Greenleaf.

The Grand Saloon was as elegant as any plantation mansion house he remembered from before the War— a large, elongated room with real carpets and crystal chandeliers. A bar ran the width of the forward bulkhead, and there a white-jacketed Negro was serving up drinks for a sizable crowd of well-dressed passengers. Slocum found Greenleaf at the far corner of the bar, watching a three-card Monte game at the nearest table.

Greenleaf took his eyes off the game just long enough to grin and shake his hand. "Be with you in a minute. Been expecting you. Got a little business to attend to first."

The Monte dealer had what looked to be a fish on the hook: a fat, flushed passenger in a Prince Albert coat, who was laying out twenty-dollar gold pieces on the turn of the cards. Slocum ordered a drink and watched over Greenleaf's shoulder. Greenleaf looked as lean and cool and wary as he remembered him, but there was a difference. He remembered him best from the last days of the War, and Greenleaf had been as drawn and haggard as they had all been then, his Reb uniform bloodied and tattered, his eyes red-rimmed above a week's growth of beard. Now he was smooth-shaven except for a dark moustache, and he wore a pair of fine-cut trousers and a knee-length broadcloth coat. Slocum couldn't see a gun, but the Greenleaf he knew would have a pistol stashed somewhere.

Now the fat passenger gathered up his winnings and went off to buy a drink at the bar, flushed and beaming. The dealer scooped up the cards, and Greenleaf turned his attention to Slocum.

"That one's bait for the suckers," he said. "Good to see you. I told the colonel he'd find you out there on that Texas plain somewhere. I see he caught up with you."

"Caught me just short of the Red River. Glad he did. You're looking good, and this sounds a lot more interesting than eating trail dust. What's with the Monte dealer?"

"I'm working for Harry Roberts, the man who owns this boat. Hired me to run off dealers cheating his passengers. Got to catch them at it first, but I'll catch this fellow."

With no takers, the dealer was switching his three cards rapidly back and forth across the table. "Watch my hands, gentlemen. All depends on the quickness of my hands. Are they faster than your eyes? One chance in three to win, gentlemen." He flicked the cards face up: a five of clubs, a six of diamonds, the ace of spades. "The ace of spades is the winning card, gentlemen." He turned the cards face down again. "Watch the ace of spades. Follow it as it moves. Pick the ace of spades and win twenty dollars. Pick the wrong card and pay me twenty. Who will wager twenty dollars? Whose eyes are faster than my hands?"

"He's good," Slocum said.

"Not good enough," Greenleaf said. "It ain't like he's dealing poker. Monte's always a crooked game."

The dealer had a new fish, a young fellow looking

as flushed as the fat man he'd replaced. He was just tossing a twenty-dollar gold piece on the table when Slocum found a beautiful woman in a satiny green gown suddenly standing at his side.

The sight of her took his breath away. She looked damned near naked in that gown. He could see the hollow of her navel in the rise of her belly. The material clung to her so tightly it was shiny around the hips; her breasts, bulging big as melons above her rib cage, came near to spilling out the top. What made it worse was that he could tell by the cool, haughty look on her face how aware she was of the effect she was having and how much she liked it: stirring a man up, in a public place, where he had to pretend not to be looking.

Watching his face with sober eyes, she laid a hand on Greenleaf's arm. "You must introduce me to your friend, Mr. Greenleaf. I will see that he's entertained while you keep an eye on the Monte dealer."

"John Slocum, ma'am," Greenleaf said. "I told you about him. John, this is Laura Roberts. Wife of the man I told you about. Owns the *River Queen*. Making the run down to New Orleans with us this trip. You keep her occupied. I got to watch this fellow here."

The young fish had already picked the ace once and won himself twenty dollars. The dealer was moving the cards in that fast sleight-of-hand again. Without taking her eyes off Slocum's face, Laura Roberts got herself a drink from the bartender, her breasts swinging heavily as she moved.

"You'll have to forgive Mr. Greenleaf," she said. "My husband's trying to clean up the gambling on this boat. I'm afraid you've walked into something."

She was watching his face as if hungry to see the

effect her appearance was having on him. He had an uneasy feeling there was something crazy about her.

"It's a nice boat," he said. "Your husband on board?"

"Mr. Roberts is already in New Orleans. I spend most of my time in St. Louis."

She hadn't smiled once yet. She was watching him over the rim of her glass, and he could see she was breathing a little hard. Her breasts rose and fell above the cut of her gown, the deep cleavage expanding and contracting. He took his eyes away and watched the Monte game.

The young fellow was winning steadily, a pile of gold pieces building up on the table in front of him. The long room was filled with the murmur of talk from the other tables, the clack of poker chips from a smoky corner, the clink of glasses at the bar. From the rear of the boat came the muffled *thump-thump* of the paddlewheels thrashing their way through the water.

The woman laid her fingers on the hand he had propped on the butt of his Colt. "Mister Greenleaf tells me you fought together in the War. Do you gamble, too?" She brought his hand up to where she could turn it and survey his palm. "I would wager you do. You have the hand of a gambler."

Slocum surveyed his big, calloused hand. "No, ma'am. That's the hand of a working man."

"I didn't mean the callouses, Mr. Slocum. I meant your palm. The character lines in your palm. Have you never had anyone read your palm?"

"No, ma'am, I can't say I have. Didn't know there was anything there to read."

"One who knows the art can read a lot in another

person's palm, Mr. Slocum. You must let me read yours."

She was looking at him with those large, inquisitive green eyes, but he caught a subtle signal from Greenleaf over by the card table. "We'll talk about it," he said. "Right now you'll have to excuse me." And he removed his hand from hers and sidled over beside Greenleaf.

The card play had stopped. There was a pile of gold pieces in front of the young fish and almost none on the other side of the table. The dealer was tapping the tabletop and studying the young fellow's face. Now he reached for an inside pocket. "You have come near to cleaning me out, my friend, but I still have a reserve here." He brought out a sack of coins and plunked it on the table. "Four thousand dollars. I will bet you the entire four thousand on one turn of the cards. Are you game? Will you go me four thousand?"

Slocum was aware of Greenleaf poised and alert beside him, of the woman's perfume in the air, of the hush that was slowly widening around the table. The young fellow flushed, licked his lips, and looked around at the crowd. Judging by the cut of his clothes, he could afford it. Now he brought out a promissory note and threw it on the table.

"I match your four thousand," he said. "Run the cards."

The dealer scanned the note, smiled, and picked up the cards. Slocum caught Greenleaf's nod and put himself where he could see both ways along the bar. The woman was a yard to one side, watching him, and the fat man who had won before was watching from the other end of the bar.

The dealer was rapidly flicking the cards back and

forth again. "Watch the cards, my friend. Watch the ace. It's a practiced art, an ancient art, the skill of the hand over the eye. One chance in three to win. Fine odds. Watch the ace. Watch the ace and pick the ace." The cards came to a stop. "Pick the ace, my friend. Pick the ace and win four thousand dollars."

The young fish reached to tap the center card. Before he could touch it, Greenleaf stepped in to grab the dealer by one wrist, a big Navy Colt in his other hand.

"Don't move," he said. "Keep your hands flat to the table. I don't want to have to shoot you."

The young fellow had jerked to the side, looking wide-eyed at Greenleaf. The dealer's face had gone white. A hush began to spread out from the table, and Slocum saw men rising from tables farther back in the room to see what was going on. Laura Roberts had moved to stand by the entrance. Now the dealer raised his eyes from the hand on his wrist to Greenleaf, trying not to look at that Colt. Slocum could hear him struggling to make his voice sound cool and easy.

"Might I know your name, sir? And what right you have to stop my game?"

"The name's Greenleaf, James Greenleaf. Just say I'm a friend of the management. Leave that hand where it is."

Slocum saw the fat man leave the corner and start along the bar, his eyes on Greenleaf's back, one hand going for what was likely a derringer in his pocket. He was in too much of a hurry to see Slocum. Slocum slipped his Colt from its holster and held it down along his thigh. When the fat man drew even with him, he whipped the Colt around and slammed it broadside into that fat belly.

The fat man gasped and grabbed for the bar, his derringer clattering to the floor. Slocum put a boot on it and stuck the muzzle of the Colt two inches deep in the fat man's belly.

"Relax. You ain't going anywhere."

The fat man was still sucking air, clinging to the bar to hold himself up. His eyes were popping, and he didn't look to have any fight now he'd lost his derringer. The Monte dealer, trying to pretend nothing had happened, was studying Greenleaf's face.

"Sir, you accuse me of cheating. If you'll allow me to turn those cards, I'll prove I'm not."

"And pull a switch while you're at it," Greenleaf said. "No, I want to see what you got up your sleeves. Young fellow, flip those cards over."

Slocum watched the young fellow turn the three cards face up on the table. A five of clubs. A six of diamonds. Another five of clubs. A low murmur passed through the crowd gathering around the table. Slowly Greenleaf turned the dealer's wrist and plucked the card peeking from under a grimy cuff. He held it up so the crowd could see: the ace of spades.

The Monte dealer tried a thin and lethal smile. "Are you quite finished?"

"Not yet." Greenleaf tossed the ace aside and patted the dealer's jacket till he found another derringer, brought it out, and tucked it into his own pocket. Then he backed away from the table, the Colt still levelled. "Put that money in your pocket, young fellow. You can figure they didn't come by it legal. You," he said to the dealer, "get back to your cabin and start packing up. You and your fat friend. You're getting put off this boat at the next woodyard."

"You're making a mistake, friend." The dealer began edging out from behind the table, holding his hands at shoulder height. "You can't stay on this boat forever. You'll have to walk the same streets I do somewhere on this run. We'll meet again."

"I'm looking forward to it," Greenleaf said. "Now take your friend and get out."

Slocum dug the muzzle of the Colt into the fat man's belly and shoved. The fat man retreated, turned, and joined the dealer on the way out, listing like a balloon with a puncture slowly leaking air. The dealer flashed one angry look over his shoulder, and then the both of them were out through the doors and the murmur of the crowd rose up in the room again.

Slocum bent to pick up the fat man's derringer and holstered the Colt. Laura Roberts was moving through the crowd, murmuring assurances, easing them all back to their tables. Greenleaf took the dealer's money sack from the young fish, pocketed it, and came over to hoist the drink the bartender had waiting for him.

"Thanks," he said. "Glad you were around. Easier to deal with the man in front of you if you don't have to worry about the man in back."

Slocum was watching the door the dealer and his shill had left through. "We didn't exactly make friends out of those two. Could be they'll try to even the score. How long before we reach the next woodyard?"

"About four hours. And you're right. I expect they're waiting out there somewhere."

"Maybe we ought to go look for them. I never liked feeling somebody was sneaking up behind me."

The crowd had drifted back to the card games around the other tables. The hum of talk settled in again, and the clack of poker chips and the murmurous voice of one man or another dealing a round of cards. Laura

Roberts returned to the bar, her long, shapely body squirming voluptuously in that tight gown. Slocum could see her watching his face, and he forced his eyes away from those bulging breasts.

She came to lean on the bar beside him, her hip pressed against his, one soft breast swelling against his arm. "Thank you, Mr. Slocum. I'm obliged to you."

"For what, ma'am?"

"For helping. I sent for a member of the crew, but he never got here." She leaned across the bar to ask the bartender for her tiny handbag, the shimmering gown tightening across the curves of her buttocks and the long line of her legs. When she straightened, her eyes went immediately to his, as if to note the effect. "I'd be grateful if you'd escort Mr. Jennings to his cabin. I'm afraid those two might attack him. I don't want to be responsible for that."

"And who's Mr. Jennings?"

"Our friend here," Greenleaf said, and waved the young fish over from the corner of the bar. "You'd better come with us, Jennings. We'll take you to your cabin." Jennings was trying to sputter his thanks, but Greenleaf cut him short. "Stay out of Monte games from now on. And best lock yourself in till we get those other two put ashore. They'll be wanting back that money they let you win."

Laura Roberts put a slim hand on Slocum's arm. "Would you please come back when you've finished there? I'll need an escort up to the pilothouse, to tell the captain we'll be stopping."

Slocum glanced from that hand to her eyes. For the first time he looked her frankly up and down: the hips round and fleshy under the sheen of her gown;

the broad hollow where the cloth stretched taut across the juncture of her thighs; those heavy breasts half-exposed above the lace of her bodice. "Yes, ma'am," he said, giving her the same blunt and challenging stare she was giving him. "Yes, ma'am, I'll be back."

3

Greenleaf told Jennings to wait at the bar while he and Slocum slipped out the door to check on things outside. Small lanterns hung along the rail stanchions, laying dim light on the polished wood deck. The black water slid quietly past below the rail. Slocum was moving to check the deck to the rear when he saw a vague figure moving toward them from the bow. He stepped back into the shadows and was reaching for his Colt when Greenleaf put out a hand to stop him.

"It's all right," Greenleaf said. "He's on our side."

The man emerged into the light—a burly deckhand Greenleaf introduced as Otis Grubb, the crewman Laura Roberts had sent for. Slocum was glad to see he looked like a man who could take care of himself. Grubb propped his broad hands on his hips, gazing at the deck and nodding while Greenleaf related what had happened in the saloon.

"Jennings is waiting inside," Greenleaf said. "I'm going to tell him you'll take him to his cabin while Slocum and I go up to the pilothouse. I expect those two are looking for him—they think he's got their money bag—so maybe we can use him as bait. You go on ahead and we'll follow."

"I take it you don't want this Jennings to know he's bait," Grubb said.

"He wouldn't be able to pull it off if he knew. Get him to talking, but keep your eyes open. Not much place to hide along these decks, but it's pretty dark. They might come out of a cabin at you."

Grubb turned to look both ways along the deck. Far out on the water the low flames of a cookfire drifted to the rear on a raft too dark to see. From the far-off bank came the baying of a hound.

"How far back you aim to be?" Grubb said.

"Got to stay back so they don't see us. We'll be close enough to pitch in."

"Don't wait too long. I got a hard head, but types like that tend to use a club."

Greenleaf went back into the saloon to bring Jennings out and told him about the change of plan. Grubb set out up the deck with him, and when they were halfway to the stairs leading down onto the main deck, Slocum and Greenleaf started along behind.

"Just so you know," Greenleaf said, "Grubb's working for me. I knew him before the War. He was working on the Roberts Riverboat line then, too. The colonel tell you what we're up to?"

"Said you were planning to hijack a boat." Slocum glanced over his shoulder, but the dimly lit deck was still empty behind them. He couldn't see a hiding place anywhere, nothing but a row of spittoons along the rail and chairs backed up against the inboard wall. "I'd feel better ambushing that shipment of repeaters the colonel's after. I don't know nothing about boats."

"Don't have to. That's why I brought Grubb into it. Grubb's going to boss the deck crew on a new Roberts boat out of New Orleans, boat called the *Gulf Queen*. She's leaving on her maiden voyage soon as we end this run. That's the boat we're taking to Mexico. Watch that corner to your left of the stairs up there."

Slocum was watching Grubb start down the stairs onto the main deck, with Jennings right behind him. The stairs were well lit, but the prow of the boiler deck bent around to the left just ahead of them. A man could hide around that corner and rush you as you went down. He listened hard, but all he could hear was the muffled thrashing of the paddlewheels and Jennings's voice drifting up from the main deck now.

"Nothing I can see. Could check it out, but Grubb would get too far ahead." They started down the stairs, watching the dark to either side. "Any boat that can work that gulf must be pretty big. I hope we got more than one man to help us."

"I told you, Grubb's bossing the deck crew. He hired them." Greenleaf halted to scan the shadowy deck at the foot of the stairs, then signalled the area was clear and led the way on toward the bow. "He knows this trade well enough to pick the right men. They're all working for us. This first trip's supposed to be special, lots of high-tone passengers aboard. I got us both hired to deal cards. You went on the payroll soon as you came aboard. We'll pick the right night out there on that gulf and take the boat over.

Watch those cotton bales along there. There'll be a big rope stacked up around this corner. Could be a place to hide."

They rounded the prow of the main deck, just aft of the bow itself and the tall flagpole rising up from it. Grubb and Jennings were moving aft now, along the deck in front of them. The rope was coiled high near a huge iron cleat just back of the bow, but he couldn't see anything out of the way there. What Greenleaf had said about passengers had taken his mind elsewhere, and he was remembering those bold green eyes, the heavy breasts, the slim waist above firm and fleshy hips in a clinging gown.

"Roberts's wife going to be on this maiden voyage? On the *Gulf Queen?*"

"I seen you looking at her. Hard not to. Yeah, she'll be aboard. She's going down now to meet Roberts in New Orleans. I don't want to tell you your business, but I'd steer clear of her. I figure she's more trouble than any two men could handle."

Slocum was watching each cabin door as they passed, waiting for one to spring open. "That just something you figure, or do you know it from experience?"

"Just speculation. Not that I think Harry Roberts would mind. They're a strange pair. He's about twenty years older than her, and I get the feeling he's put all his manhood in the boat business. Like maybe the only way he can take any pleasure of her is seeing her do like she was tonight. She flaunts herself like that even when he's on board. Seems to take special pleasure in it then. You can fair see her eyes glitter. Never seen her take a man to bed, but I've watched her make enough of them want her real bad. Gets them all twisted up till their eyes bug out."

Up ahead, Grubb and Jennings had stopped at a cabin door, and Jennings was fumbling in his pocket for the key. Slocum stopped to give their quarry room to move if they were going to, and Greenleaf put himself against a door opposite the rail. The only sound was the ripple of the water sliding quietly past and the dull thrashing of the paddlewheels beating away toward the stern. Still nobody in sight.

"Maybe they gave it up," Slocum said.

"I wouldn't count on it." Greenleaf turned his back to the wind to light a cigar. "They figure he's got that money sack. Likely they've been watching from somewhere and seen us and Grubb. Could be they'll wait and see if they can get in there when he's alone."

Jennings had the door unlocked. Grubb moved him aside and pushed into the cabin, likely to make sure it was empty. Slocum saw the flare of a match and the glow of a lamp coming from inside, but Jennings was still hanging back out on the deck. His own mind was still on the woman, thinking how that fleshy body would look sprawled naked on the bed in her stateroom, wondering just how much of that challenge in her eyes was real, if it was all just meant to torment a man or if there was something more. Likely, Greenleaf was right. Likely she had nothing but trouble to offer. But a month spent driving cattle across Texas could make a man put his judgement away for a while.

Now he saw Grubb come back out of the cabin and wave them on. The door had closed behind him, cutting off the light, leaving Jennings inside.

"Looks like they're waiting," Greenleaf said. "Let's go talk things over."

Grubb was stuffing a pinch of tobacco in his cheek

when they got to him. He put the tobacco can in his rear pocket and wiped his fingers on his pants. "Your friends never showed. You think they know something we don't know?"

"Could be," Greenleaf said. "They know this run. They know where the next woodyard is. They ain't going to just sit around waiting to be put off. Not without making a play for that money."

Slocum took the makings out of his vest pocket and started crimping up the paper for a smoke. "You think they might have a friend or two?"

"That ain't impossible, either," Greenleaf said. "Likely we ought to do a little hunting. We can leave Jennings. He ain't going to let anybody in till we tell him it's all right."

"Let's go find the purser," Grubb said. "He can tell us where their cabin is, anyway. Maybe they're still there plotting strategy. It's another three hours at least to that woodyard."

"That's what I need a boat man for," Greenleaf said. "The purser's something I'd never have thought of. Let's go see what he has to say."

"Just a minute," Slocum said. "I got to finish rolling this smoke."

He had wet the paper down and was just twisting it up tight when a burst of noise behind him brought his head around. Three dark shapes were springing out of the next cabin over. He just had time to drop the cigarette before something struck his skull so hard he went black even before he fell.

4

He was in a giant bell, in the dark inside it, and the bell had just been set ringing. He could feel the vibrations from it in his head. He couldn't see, and his mouth was dry, and his mind wouldn't work. Every time he tried to speak, another iron vibration rang through him, leaving him too weak to move. Then something touched his head, something real, something cold, and he yanked himself upright, remembering.

"Whoa," somebody said. "Take it easy. No hurry now."

Carefully, he eased himself back down and opened his eyes.

Greenleaf was leaning over him. They were in a cabin, not his own, a cabin big enough to be called a stateroom, and he was lying on a bed. He could hear the paddlewheels thrashing back near the stern, could feel them vibrating through the boat, through the bed, and through his head. And now he remembered it: the black night on the portside deck, crimping up a cigarette, the three men bursting out of that cabin door.

He swallowed once and got some of his voice back. "What happened?"

"They suckered us," Greenleaf said. "Had a friend spotting the game through a saloon window. He saw me pocket that money sack and crossed over the Texas deck to tell the first two. They forced their way into that cabin. Already knew where Jennings's cabin was. One of them bent a good-sized club over your head."

"I figured that." Slocum brought a hand up to probe gingerly at his scalp. The hand came away wet, but it didn't seem to be blood. "You take care of them? You put them ashore?"

"Only got one to put ashore. Believe it or not, Jennings heard the ruckus and pitched in. When they saw us getting the best of them, the first two went over the side. Jumped overboard and struck out for land. Grubb's got the other one tied up in the purser's office."

Slocum felt the mattress shift under him and turned to see Laura Roberts on the other edge of the bed, dipping a cloth in a bowl of water in her lap. He saw a door into what looked to be a sitting room beyond her, and it dawned on him that he was in Harry Roberts's stateroom, lying on Roberts's bed with the man's wife sitting half out of her clothes not two feet away. Every swell and hollow of her body showed through that tight satiny gown, and when she leaned to put the damp cloth to his head he could see both swelling breasts all the way to her nipples.

"I'm going up to the pilothouse," Greenleaf said.

"Got to tell the captain to stop at that woodyard. You rest easy. I'll see you in the morning."

When Greenleaf was gone, Laura Roberts went to put the bowl on a dressing table against the opposite wall. She turned in time to catch his eyes on the line of her legs and the curves of her buttocks, so clear under that tight gown.

"Please take your boots off, Mr. Slocum. You're dirtying my bed."

That surprised him, and he didn't like her officious tone, but she seemed to mean it. "Yes, ma'am." He shucked his boots and lay back on the pillow.

She bent to remove some frothy female underthing from a chair, giving him a flash of deep cleavage between jiggling breasts so big and full they seemed to glow. She flicked him a cool, inquisitive glance and turned to stuff the frothy garment in a drawer. He was beginning to resent the show she was putting on. At least a whore was willing to let you have what she was offering. Greenleaf was right. This kind of woman offered only trouble.

Now she was standing in profile to him, hands propped in the small of her back, arching like she had a sudden need to take the kinks out of her spine. Then she tossed her hair back from her shoulders and flicked that quick glance at him again.

"I trust that means you're feeling better?" she asked.

"What's that, ma'am?"

"The way you're looking at me."

He didn't know what to make of that. The tone of her voice was cool and superior, and that sober look on her face was hardly inviting. Only the heavy-lidded eyes gave any hint there was more going on inside her than she showed.

"A little hard not to," he said.

"Perhaps you should make more of an effort." She came around to test the dampness of the cloth on his head, bending so that again he could see both breasts bare to the nipples. "I had you brought here where it's comfortable," she said, cool and detached as any nurse. "I didn't invite you to stare at me."

"Maybe you'll explain something then. The way you're standing right now, I can see halfway down that gown. You tell me what that is if it's not an invitation."

"You're on my husband's boat, Mr. Slocum. I do as I please here. I dress as I please, and I stand as I please. Anyone who objects can leave the boat."

She hadn't moved. She was still testing the cloth on his head, still bending to display her big, bare breasts only inches from his eyes. Watching him, her eyes heavy-lidded, she flicked her tongue out to wet her lips, and her mouth stayed slightly open now, full and wet and glistening. Her nipples were growing larger—rising, stiffening—and the sound of her breathing told him how much pleasure she got from twisting a man up like this.

She seemed to want an answer, some proof of the effect she was having. "If you can't keep your eyes to yourself, Mr. Slocum, you have a problem. Remember, you work for me."

"I work for your husband. At least, I did." He tossed the damp cloth onto the bedspread, rolled off the bed, and got to his feet. "Not sure I want to hang around where I have to look at you."

"You find looking at me unpleasant?" She was standing so close he could see right down into her gown, but still she wouldn't move.

"Not the looking, no."

"You'll have less trouble if you remember your place, Mr. Slocum." She bent to pluck the damp cloth off the bed. "You have a very direct stare. In polite circles you would not be called a gentleman."

"And you got a cruel streak a mile wide, lady. In any circle I know, you'd be called a whore."

She jerked like he'd hit her and wheeled up from the bed, bringing an open hand around in a wild swing toward his face. He caught her by the wrist, and she twisted and tried to slap him with her other hand, but he caught that wrist, too, holding her while she squirmed and struggled, heavy breasts jiggling in the scoop of her gown. Then she stopped, head down like she was gathering strength for another try, and he became aware of her groin pressed up against his.

He couldn't see her eyes, couldn't tell if it was the struggle that had brought her up against him like that, but she made no move to pull away. For a moment she remained poised there, breathing hard, then she writhed up again, whimpering furiously, struggling to free her wrists. When she subsided again, she still had her groin pressed against his. He was up hard and erect.

Slowly, he bent her arms behind her back till he could seize both wrists in one hand. Then he forced her head up with the other. "You see, you got what you wanted."

She kept her head turned as far away as she could, watching him with the wild and hostile eyes of an animal. Her breasts rose and fell with her breathing.

"That wasn't all you wanted, was it?" he said, and ripped her gown down to her waist, watching those huge breasts lurch out, big-nippled, bouncing in the open air.

She cried out then, twisting and struggling in his grasp. She tried to bring a knee up into his crotch, but he blocked it and pushed her back till her legs were pinned against the side of the bed. She writhed a moment or two longer and then subsided again, her head turned away, her hair falling down to shield her face. She was taut as a coiled spring, so hot now he could smell her. Her huge breasts were heaving, the nipples large and erect.

"I think we ought to give you everything you wanted." He seized the cloth at her waist and yanked, and the whole gown came away in his hand. He wasn't surprised to find she wore nothing under it.

He had an armful of voluptuous, squirming flesh. She fought him every way she could—driving a hip into his groin, butting him with her head, lashing suddenly down to bite at his arm. Her eyes were clenched shut the whole time, and she seemed almost maniacally strong, but he could feel the warmth of her through his clothes, and her nipples stayed large and hard, and the smell of her was strong as any animal in heat. He could hear genuine rage in her whimpers, but she didn't once try to scream.

Now she got a leg free and tried to twist loose, but that only put her off balance. He drove one hip against hers and toppled her back on the bed, landing between her thighs, still gripping her wrists behind her back with one hand. She dug her heels into the bed and tried to propel herself out from under him, but his grip was too strong, and all she could do was arch up and twist and collapse again while he fumbled with his belt and kicked his pants down. He forced her knees wider apart and rose up and entered that warm, wet opening between her thighs.

He didn't do it fast. He held her wrists behind her with both hands now. He was propped on his own wrists and his knees, just far enough inside her to keep from being dislodged. For a moment she lay there, trembling with what he knew was something close to rage. Slowly, he inched deeper into her. She caught herself then and reared up on her shoulders and feet, trying to throw him off, but he moved when she moved, keeping himself where he was. She stayed poised in midair for five seconds, quivering; then her strength gave out and she collapsed onto the bed, but he stayed with her again, following her down so that even that violent movement brought him only another inch deeper into her. She had barely hit the bed before she lunged upward again, and this time he held himself rigid, letting the lunge of her own body impale her on him.

Again she shuddered in midair and arched up off the bed. When she collapsed this time he drove hard into her, all the way to the hilt.

Her feet were propped against the bed, her body rigid with resistance, but she was soft and moist and warm inside, and he knew she would break, knew she would give. He kept plunging rhythmically into her, timing his strokes to the beat of her breathing, and soon he felt some of the tension leave her muscles, felt the resistance slacken, felt that rigid arch began to sag. Now her upper body began slowly to rock, her hips relaxed, her thighs began to sag apart; deep guttural sounds began coming from her now, pulled from her reluctant throat by the force of that pleasure he was driving into her. He felt her rump begin to move under his arms. Her hips began to twitch. Her body began to writhe again, but not with resistance now, with need, with pleasure, with slowly growing abandon. With a fierce relentless hunger that soon matched and then surpassed the fury of her resistance, till she was struggling hard as before to free her arms— not now in order to flee, but for what she did when he did release them: flung her hands out wide above her head and clenched the bedspread and arched that supple torso up, huge big-nippled breasts bobbing under his eyes as her hips lunged and drove against his, powerfully, frantically, each frantic, lunging stroke accompanied by those deep and fiercely animal cries. Now her arms came down around him like a trap and she lost all hold of earth and was gone, wriggling like a woman gone mad, that voluptuous naked flesh squirming against his till he felt her go over, heard the sound of it in her cry, felt it rise immediately up and crest in her again and again, the cries coming continuously from her now till the sound and feel of her seized him out of himself and he was no longer aware of anything but sensation.

The first thing he was aware of was the tiny ticking of a watch. He was drenched with sweat. The heat was slowly draining out of his brain, and he realized he was still half dressed and hearing the ticking of the stemwinder in his vest pocket. He was lying between her legs, unwilling to move. He opened his eyes and saw her flung out on the bed. From the sound of her breathing, she might have been asleep. He rolled off her, stripped off what remained of his clothes, and wiped his face on his shirt.

"You can get out now," she said.

She hadn't opened her eyes. She hadn't moved.

He rose up on one elbow. "I don't think I heard you right. Maybe you better say that again."

"You've served your purpose. Now get out."

He seized the hair at the nape of her neck and forced her to turn her head. She made no move to resist—almost as if to show how unimportant he was—but she gave him a look so intense it might have been hate he saw in her eyes.

"Let me tell you something," he said. "I don't let people talk to me that way. No man ever has without paying pretty high, and no man ever will. I've never hurt a woman, but I can if it's called for. You understand me?"

She lay there limp in his grasp, looking him dead in the face with those baleful eyes, and nothing he'd said seemed to have disconcerted her a bit. His grip in her hair pulled the skin of her face back and caused her eyes and her mouth to go slitted till she looked almost Oriental. He took a long, deliberate look up and down that shapely body, then he let her head drop.

"You got me in here for one thing. And I'll leave when I please. I might take orders from your husband. I don't take orders from you."

He reached for his vest and began fingering his tobacco sack out of the pocket.

5

"How many do you count?" Lewis said.

Squinting against the sun, his elbows propped in the dirt, Lieutenant Brown returned his field glasses to his eyes and scanned the U.S. Army wagon train rolling along the south Texas desert below.

"Nineteen mounted troopers," Brown said. "Plus the captain in command. Four wagons. Four mule skinners."

"Same count I have," Lewis said. "Unless there's a man or two in those wagons, we have twenty-four against us."

He and Brown were lying on their bellies at the crest of a narrow, sandy ridge just south of the plain the wagon train was crossing. The ridge, treeless and without cover of any kind, stretched away to the west as far as Lewis could see. Behind him, holding the horses at the bottom of the slope, were his own men—eight refugees from the Carlota Colony and two who, like Brown, had fought under him during the War. He adjusted his own field glasses and went back to examining the wagon train.

A twenty-man cavalry detachment. And according to rumors he'd picked up in the shantytown around Camp Smith, where the detachment had left from, all of them bound for the Mexican border to rendezvous with troops of Benito Juarez. Escorting four wagon-loads of weapons—sixteen-shot Henry repeaters with several thousand rounds of ammunition—crated and ready for delivery. Through the glasses he could see the troopers carried seven-shot Spencer carbines along with their sidearms. And he had twelve men, counting himself, armed with muzzle-loaders left over from the War. They were not only outnumbered, but outgunned.

"We can't attack them in force," he said. "We'll have to trail them till they bed down, then take them when they're asleep. Put a scout up here to keep an eye on them, but make sure he's not seen."

"I'll detail Corporal Hodges," Brown said. "He's had scouting experience."

They trailed the wagon train for the rest of the afternoon, staying on the south side of the ridge, paralleling the detachment's route of march. Shortly after sundown, Hodges angled his horse down the slope and signalled with his hat. Lewis left his horse with Brown and climbed the ridge on foot to where Hodges had dismounted and wriggled his way up to the crest.

"They're making camp," Hodges said. "Down in that arroyo."

Lewis brought his field glasses up again. The cavalry captain had pulled the wagons down into a deep arroyo winding off to the southwest, putting them out of sight of anybody approaching along the plain. The mule skinners had unhitched the mules and were leading them to a spot forward of the wagons, where three of the troopers were already picketing the cavalry mounts. Several others were building fires for evening chow. Four guards had been posted, up on the banks of the arroyo, two near the front of the wagons, two at the rear, far enough out to give alarm before any intruders got close.

"Keep watch till you're sure they don't change that formation any," Lewis said. "I'm going to bed our men down, too. I'll send a man up to spell you in two hours. We'll take them after midnight."

He had Brown select enough men to relieve each other every two hours up on the ridge and posted two guards of his own. They could light no fires for fear of the glow being seen from down on the plain; after a supper of cold rations, Lewis rolled up in his bedroll and was immediately asleep. He was dreaming of the Carlota Colony, of the Confederate Hotel in Cordoba, where the colony had held its cotillions and where the bar was tended by a mess boy who had once served Stonewall Jackson, when someone shook him awake. He came up on one elbow to see it was Lieutenant Brown.

"It's time," Brown said. "You said to wake you at one. The men are already up."

Lewis rubbed the sleep from his eyes and sat up in his bedroll. His bones ached. He was getting too old for sleeping out on bare ground. He searched his blankets for his canteen, took a swallow, and poured out a handful to splash on his face. Once on his feet, he found his mind clear and alert, already working on the problem of the wagon train. It was good to feel like a military man again.

"Anything changed down in the arroyo?" he asked the lieutenant.

"Not that I can see," Brown said. "The fires have gone out, but the moon's fairly bright. *Too* bright. Those guards will spot us before we're halfway to them. Only way I can see is to ride down off that bluff at a gallop. Maybe that way we can take the guards out before the others get organized."

"I've got a better idea," Lewis said. "Have the men gather round."

From off in the dark around him he could hear the vague sounds of sleepy men gathering up their bedrolls, the slosh of water in the canteen on somebody's belt, a muffled curse as one man tripped on a rock. A pale quarter moon hung in the black sky overhead. He had just pulled his boots on when Brown brought the men to hunker down in a semicircle in front of him.

"I've pulled the sentries in," Brown said.

"Good," Lewis said. "Now listen up. We're going to go on about another three hundred yards west. That arroyo swings in to run along the bottom of the ridge on the other side there. That's where we'll cross over. We'll leave the horses on this side and go over afoot. If we can get down into that arroyo without being seen, we ought to be able to catch those troopers in their beds before the guards even know we're there."

"We're still outnumbered two to one," Brown said.

"That won't matter if things go right," Lewis said. "Take only your sidearms when we leave the horses. Rifles would just get in the way. And leave anything that might make noise in your bedroll. Any of you with canteens on your belts, anybody with spurs on, take them off. We're going to have to get right in amongst them while they're still sleeping."

When the men had their bedrolls lashed on behind their saddles, they mounted up and Lewis started them west at a walk. The ridge, worn by wind and weather, meandered snakelike across the desert. Stars winked in the black sky overhead, and the night was cool after the heat of the day. The only sounds were the quiet thump of hooves on hard ground, the creak of saddle leather, the occasional snort of a horse. When Lewis figured they'd covered a good three hundred yards, he signalled a halt and dismounted.

"Keep it quiet," he said. "Never tell how far sounds will carry on a desert at night like this. Hodges, you stay here with the horses. You hear any shooting start, bring them over at a run. We'll likely need them. Otherwise, hold them here, and when we've got things under control, I'll give you one shot as a signal to come on over. Everybody ready?"

"We're ready, sir," Brown said.

"Good. We'll go up and take a look first. Remember, no canteens, no spurs, nothing that'll make any noise. And sidearms only. All right, let's go."

When he neared the crest, he got down on his belly and crawled up to where he could see down the other side. Brown was just to his right, the other men bunched up behind him. Lewis had left his field glasses on his horse, but even without them he could see the white canvas tops of the wagons bulging up out of the arroyo a hundred yards or so to the northeast. Moonlight reflected off the desert itself so that he could see the dark shapes of the sentries, two in front, two to the rear. He couldn't see the animals, but unless they'd been moved, they would be down in that arroyo, ahead of the wagons, just about between those first two sentries.

He rolled half on his side so he could whisper to the men behind him. "We'll have to go down one at a time. Moon's bright, but we'll be in the shadow of the ridge till we reach the arroyo, so we ought to be all right. Brown, you go first. Then the rest of you. I'll come last. Hold up down there till we're all together again."

Brown took a long look at where those sentries were posted out on the flat to either side of the arroyo. Then he elbowed his way over the crest and started working his way down the north face of the ridge. Lewis watched him till he was out of sight in the moon shadow. He waited till even the faint scrape of Brown's boots had faded, then waved the next man up and over. All the time he kept his eyes on those sentries out on the flat, scanned the arroyo around the area of the wagon tops, and kept his ears cocked for any unexpected sound.

He felt good, commanding troops again, out in the night under the moon, going in harm's way, with nothing but his nerve and his men and a Dance revolver to stand between him and whatever danger was waiting out there. He waved the last man up and over the crest. When that man had been out of sight and sound for what he calculated to be two minutes, he tugged his hat low over his brow and started bellying down the ridge himself.

He found Brown and the others crouched in the dark when he crawled over the edge of the arroyo and dropped down in with them. The dry channel was half in darkness and half in moonlight. He drew his revolver again and checked to see it hadn't picked up any sand.

"Let's move out. I'll take the lead. Brown, you bring up the rear."

Crouching now, he moved on up the dark arroyo. It bent and switched back on itself every few yards, so that he had to shift from side to side to stay out of the moonlight. Hodges was right behind him, the others strung out single file behind Hodges. Again Lewis felt that surge in his chest, the joy of being back in your element, doing what you'd been born and bred to do. He heard a faint noise up ahead and halted and held up a hand. After a second or two he saw it was a toad of some kind, moving in staggering hops through the sand. When it had passed into shadow, he moved on.

Soon the arroyo began to angle north. He knew they were approaching the place where those troopers had picketed the animals. He slowed his pace to a crawl, watching the dark in front of him. Finally, easing his head around a bend to the right, he saw a shapeless black cluster up ahead: the mules and the cavalry mounts, barely distinguishable in the dark. About thirty yards beyond the animals were the wagons, and to the right of the wagons he could see the dark lumps which were the troopers lying asleep in their bedrolls.

He waited till the others had crowded up behind him. "Mules are just ahead," he whispered. "Wagons about thirty yards beyond that. Troopers sleeping beside the wagons. This is the tricky part. I'm going to crawl ahead and find their captain and put a pistol to his head. Once I've done that, move through those bedrolls quiet as you can and take every man's weapon."

"Maybe you better let one of us go," Brown said. "That's no job for the man in command."

"This isn't the army anymore," Lewis said. "If something goes wrong, likely none of us will survive, anyway. And make sure you check those wagons. Somebody might be sleeping in them."

"You going to wake the captain?"

"Not till you've got all their weapons. I'll bring him awake then and have him wake his men. One by one, so we can handle them."

Hodges glanced nervously toward the sleeping troopers. "What if somebody wakes up and starts shooting?"

"Just pray nobody does. I'll try to get the captain awake in time to stop anything, but we'll just have to deal with it as it comes. We'll have surprise, anyway. We have a good chance."

"I still think you ought to let one of us go in first," Brown said.

"We'll do it my way. Once you've got their weapons, spread out where you can cover them all at once. I want them to see nothing but gun muzzles when they come awake. Any questions?"

Nobody said anything.

"All right. Stick tight till I wave you up. And take it very slow. You don't want to spook the animals. And remember, those sentries are about thirty yards out on both sides."

He moved on cautiously up the arroyo. The animals were picketed in a bunch on the left, one sleeping mule angled out so it almost blocked the way. Lewis turned his back to the opposite bank and squeezed past, careful to avoid one uptilted rear hoof. When he got within twenty yards of the wagons, he went down on his belly and crawled forward till he was within reach of the first bedroll beside the front wagon.

A pair of boots stood beside the blankets. A rifle and a holstered pistol lay near the boots. The man's arm was flung out of the blankets—a sergeant, judging by the chevrons on the sleeve. Lewis moved to the next bedroll.

This man was too tightly rolled in his blankets to show any sleeve. Beside the bedroll was another pair of boots, a rifle and a pistol, and an officer's wide-brimmed campaign hat. Lewis held the hat up to the faint moonlight and saw by the captain's insignia that he had found his man. He rose to his knees, holding his pistol an inch or two away from the captain's ear, and turned to wave the others forward.

They crept up out of the dark, Brown in the lead. Brown cast a quick glance at the captain, then removed the man's rifle and pistol. Hodges removed the sergeant's weapons, took the captain's from Brown, and crawled over to lay them under the first wagon. The other men were moving slow and cautious through the bedrolls. hoisting rifles and pistols and knives and passing them over to be laid under the same wagon. Lewis held his breath, keeping one eye on the sleeping captain, silently praying it wasn't time for those sentries out there to be relieved.

When the last of the weapons had been gathered up, Brown and the others rose ghostlike from the far side of the bedrolls and began forming up alongside the wagons. Lewis saw they had replaced their muzzle-loaders with repeaters taken from the sleeping troopers and made a mental note to commend Brown for that piece of thinking. Now the troopers were covered by ten Spencer carbines. Lewis brought the muzzle of his pistol up about even with the captain's cheekbone and shook him with the other hand.

"*Hsst*. Captain. Wake up."

The captain was instantly awake. He turned his head toward the sound of Lewis's voice and started to rise. Then he saw the gun muzzle only an inch from his eyes. He froze where he was.

"Don't make a sound," Lewis whispered. "Take a look by the wagons. You're disarmed and surrounded. Take your time. Get your head clear. You're the first one shot if there's any trouble."

Slowly, like maybe that pistol was some vicious animal he didn't dare take his eyes off for long, the captain turned his head away till he saw Brown and the others ranked along the wagons. Then, just as slowly, he looked at Lewis again.

"You don't plan very well, Captain," Lewis said. "You got guards everywhere except where it counts— where they can see you. Now you be very careful. I want you to start waking your men. One by one. Tell them just to sit tight and cause no trouble. They've all been disarmed, anyway."

The captain was studying him in what little light there was. "What happens when I get my men awake?"

"Then you call your guards in. Then we take your wagons."

"It's the rifles, is it?"

"That's right. Four wagonloads of Henry repeaters. The army's got a lot of them. It's nothing to die over.

You ready to do things my way?"

The captain lay back in his bedroll, looking at the sky. Finally, he nodded.

"Good," Lewis said. "That's a good command decision. Now get those men awake."

The captain swore once under his breath, then rolled up out of his blankets. He shook his men awake one by one, bringing each carefully out of sleep so that none would panic and alarm those sentries. Only one trooper, a blond-haired youngster fresh from a farm somewhere, showed fright when he saw the carbines pointed at him, but a low, sharp word from the captain calmed him down. Lewis had to admit the captain was a good officer, cool and quick to do the necessary, and obviously respected by his men.

When they were all awake, Lewis sat them in a circle beside the lead wagon, their backs to one another, and had the captain call the sentries in, making each sentry stand and drop his weapons and come in alone. He added them to the circle, along with their captain, and fired off a round to bring Hodges with the horses.

Brown set a man to loading the troopers' weapons into the wagons and came over to join him. "A first-class operation, Colonel." He was grinning, obviously pleased with himself. "Feels good. Like being in the War again."

"You did a good job, Lieutenant." For the first time now, Lewis felt the strain. He was sweating, though the night was cool. Maybe Brown had been right; maybe his desire to take the lead was foolish bravado a real army would wisely have denied him. "Detail four men to hitch the wagons up. We'll take their mounts with us."

"You can't leave us afoot out here."

Lewis sought in the circle for the man who had spoken and was surprised to learn it was the captain; it was the first time he'd heard the man speak aloud.

"You don't think I'm going to leave you mounts to chase us with, do you? We'll want your uniforms, too. Start stripping down to your underwear."

A chorus of protest came from the circle now. The captain got to his feet— a brave act; three guards were holding carbines on him—and advanced on Lewis. Lewis waved away a guard about to force the man back to his place. The captain halted in front of him, almost at attention, almost courtly. Lewis realized it was the Rebel coat he wore: the courtesy of one officer to another.

"You can't mean what you're saying," the captain said. "Without clothing to keep the sun off, without horses, without water, we'll die out here. If that is your intention, sir, you may as well shoot us now."

"You can wear your blankets," Lewis said. "Dress yourselves like Arabs. It's said to be cooler and more efficient in desert country, anyway. And you have water on the wagons. I'll leave you two barrels. That should see you off the desert. Now, I want whatever orders you carry. And, I assure you, for the slightest trouble I *will* have you shot. I cannot afford the niceties of war."

Hodges was bringing the horses down into the arroyo, a rolling river of noise. One team of mules was already hitched to a wagon. Three more were being backed into place. The captain stood there a moment longer, looking at Lewis. Then he pulled an envelope from an inside pocket, handed it over, and went back to his men. When Lewis was sure they were stripping, he opened the envelope and struck a match to see what he had.

The man's army papers identified him as Captain William Jones. There was a set of temporary-duty orders detaching him from Camp Smith, a separate set of orders for the men under his command, and a letter on the official stationery of Philip Sheridan, Commanding General, Division of the Missouri. The letter declared the bearer, Captain William Jones, to be on special secret assignment by order of the commanding general himself, and directed all persons of authority, whether military or civil, to grant Captain Jones every assistance, without question or hindrance, in the furtherance of his mission.

Lewis caught Captain Jones watching him. Yes, the army had plenty of wagons and lots of rifles. Jones would no doubt return to Camp Smith for more, and Juarez would be none the poorer. Jones could get another letter from Sheridan, too. But this one would be useful to anybody ferrying a wagon train of stolen weapons halfway across Texas. Lewis returned the papers to the envelope and tucked it into his tunic pocket.

He had the troopers' uniforms stowed in the lead wagon and set them down again in that circle, back to back, in their underwear now. The teams were hitched up, four of his own men on the wagon seats as mule skinners. He watched Hodges and another man tying the troopers' mounts and those of the mule skinners on a lead rope behind the rear wagon. Things were going well. He had lost the feeling of strain. Back again was that pleasure at being active once more out under a starlit sky, with the happy sights and sounds of his own men moving quickly and efficiently to wrap up a successful assault.

Brown came out of the dark, leading Lewis's horse and his own. "We're ready to go, sir. I had the men leave off two water barrels. Hodges says he thinks he saw a place just below the ridge where we can get the wagons out of the arroyo."

"Good," Lewis said. "Give him my compliments. I didn't even think to look."

Brown was looking at those half-clad men in the circle in the sand. "Carrying those barrels will slow them down. We should have no trouble reaching Corpus Christi before they can give warning."

"We've been lucky." Lewis took his horse and swung into the saddle. "Let's hope luck favors Slocum and Greenleaf, as well. All this was for nothing if there's no boat waiting when we reach Corpus Christi."

6

The streets were crowded near the docks. The hansom cab clip-clopped along the cobbles, dodging buggies and private carriages and freight wagons leaving the piers. The driver yanked the team out around another cab, and Slocum had to grab for a window stanchion to stay upright. New Orleans hack drivers were as bad as any mule skinner he'd ever ridden with in Texas.

"There's the *Gulf Queen*," Greenleaf said. "Pride of the Roberts line. Bound for all the ports down the Texas coast."

Slocum saw her up ahead on the right, a long, low ship parallel to the dock, with a pair of covered paddlewheels looking huge amidships. Two tall masts rose up in a maze of rigging, and forward of the superstructure he could see twin smokestacks gleaming black in the morning sunlight.

"Let's hope she's seaworthy," he said. "She's got a long way to go. A lot longer than Roberts is planning on."

The cab pulled up behind a row of carriages at the gangplank, and Slocum got the baggage down while Greenleaf paid the driver. The *Gulf Queen* loomed overhead, looking a lot bigger up close. Fashionably dressed passengers climbed the gangplank, and a couple dozen more were already strolling around on deck. What looked to be slabs of lumber dangled from a cargo hoist near the bow, and Slocum saw some of Grubb's deck crew hauling on a rope up there, taking the load on board.

Stuffing a roll of bills in his pocket, Greenleaf came over to take his bag. "Well," he said, looking up at the people on deck, "let's go meet the fancy folk."

Harry and Laura Roberts were greeting passengers at the head of the gangplank. Slocum had met Harry Roberts once before, when the *River Queen* had docked in New Orleans, but the big, bluff, white-haired man had paid him no more mind then than he did now. Laura Roberts was dressed a sight more sensible than she had been on the *River Queen*, but even a full skirt and a high lace collar couldn't hide that voluptuous figure.

"Please come back on deck when you've unpacked," she said. "We're having a reception before sailing, and we want you to mingle with the passengers."

Only the blunt look in her eyes showed there had ever been anything between them, and then she turned to the next passenger and even that was no longer visible.

A steward directed Slocum to his cabin. It was

back near the paddlewheels but a lot better than he'd expected, fairly large and with a full-sized bed. He wondered if Laura Roberts had picked it out. After that first time, he'd ignored her on the *River Queen*. He figured that must have roused her ire, because the night before reaching New Orleans she'd slipped into his cabin, a vague and scented form he'd sensed more than seen in the dark beside the door. When he'd tried to touch her she'd fought as hard as she had the first time, and when that violent wrestling on the bed had wrenched release from her again she'd lain silent in the dark till he was damned near asleep and then rose and dressed and left the cabin without ever saying a word. From the look in her eyes just now he figured she'd be visiting this bed before the trip was over. He wasn't sure how he felt about that.

He unpacked and put his things away and in the mirror checked his new outfit—a black broadcloth coat, gray trousers above black boots, a pearl-gray Stetson that had cost twice what the coat had—then went out to meet Greenleaf.

Back on deck they got a drink from the bar set up just aft of the gangplank and worked their way through the fancy-dressed passengers till they could slip away and find Grubb. Grubb was up on a crate supervising the loading of cargo into a hatch back of the bow. When he saw them sheltering back of a large vent on deck he handed his megaphone to another deckhand and came down off his perch.

"Everything's squared away," he said. "'Less you count the passengers, there's more of us than there is of them. We should have no trouble with them."

"Who we got to worry about?" Slocum said.

"Engine crew and officers. That's not counting passengers. We do it at night, after midnight, say, the shift on duty in the engine room's the only problem. There'll be a man or two in the pilothouse, but everybody else'll be sacked out."

"Pick your two best men and bring them to my cabin after midnight tonight," Greenleaf said. "I want to talk things over. We want to figure out the easiest way of doing it. No sense giving ourselves more trouble than we have to."

"I'll bring Wilson and Brooks," Grubb said. "They're smart and they're tough. And they already know this boat like their mother's kitchen."

"That's the kind we want," Greenleaf said. "Better get back to work now. Don't want Roberts to see us too chummy."

When Grubb had climbed back onto his crate and started bellowing orders again, Slocum and Greenleaf skirted back around toward the reception going on near the gangplank.

"When you figure on doing it?" Slocum said.

"If things go right, Lewis plans to meet us at Corpus Christi," Greenleaf said. "We're going to need time to straighten things out and put the passengers ashore first. I'd say best time is two nights before we reach Corpus Christi."

At midnight two nights before the *Gulf Queen* was set to reach Corpus Christi, Slocum lay drained and drenched with sweat on the bed in his cabin. He sensed Laura Roberts lying sprawled and naked beside him, could hear her still breathing heavily from the strain of what had just ended between them. Neither of them had said a word since she'd slipped into the cabin an hour earlier. The only sounds had been her furious whimpering as he'd fought her to a reluctant surrender, the violent animal sounds of that brutal mating on the bed, her throaty outcries toward the end. It had been like this every night since the *Gulf Queen* had left New Orleans. And every day after, she had been as cool and aloof as if he were simply another hired hand, just another dealer hired to play cards with the passengers. He didn't pretend to understand her, and he still thought she was a little crazy. But if all went well, these nightly visits could turn out to be useful, in more ways than one. This particular visit especially.

Now he heard her leave the bed, heard the sounds of her dressing in the dark. She always left in silence; this time he was surprised to hear her voice coming from somewhere between him and the door. "Come to my stateroom tomorrow afternoon," she said. "About five. Just before dinner."

He was so surprised—at what she wanted, at the fact that she'd spoken at all—that he didn't answer. He could sense her leaning over the bed now, as if trying to sense him in the dark.

"Harry'll be playing poker with the captain and the rest of the men." The sound of her breathing was loud in the darkness. "I want to do it there. On our bed. On his bed."

The idea struck his brain a little numb. He had a sudden image of the two of them naked and struggling on Harry Roberts's bed—the heat of it and the animal cries—and Roberts himself coming in to find them that way. Likely it was the risk that excited her. Or maybe Roberts knew about it, and it was for Roberts she wanted to do it: to stimulate the old man when all else failed.

SOUTH OF THE BORDER 59

When he didn't answer, she said, "Did you hear me?"

"I heard you. You may be crazy. That don't mean I have to be. Find somebody else."

Her silence told him how she'd taken that—like a slap in the face. "I'll have you put off this boat," she said.

He curbed the urge to say something cruel, curbed the urge to rise and strike her. He knew where that would lead—to another struggle and back to bed. She was still hovering over him. He could almost feel the heat of her eyes on him, angry and combative. He was glad this was almost over. Soon he would be rid of her, rid of the desire he felt for her even now.

Now she turned and moved away in the dark. "Tomorrow afternoon," she said. "You know where."

When he heard the door close, he swung quickly out of bed, threw his clothes on, and went out into the companionway. A dim glow filtered down from a coal-oil light fixture at the top of a staircase farther forward. A vague figure approached out of the dark on his right, and he felt a man's hand touch his arm. Greenleaf.

"You see her come out?" Slocum said.

"She just went up those stairs," Greenleaf said. "I got Grubb and his boys waiting in place. Let's get after her."

Staying as quiet as possible, they hurried on along the companionway and up the stairs onto the deck. Blue moonlight showed a choppy sea out past the deck rail. She was nowhere in sight; it wasn't till they'd entered the companionway leading to the fancier staterooms that Slocum saw her up ahead, in the dim glow of another light fixture somewhere around a corner beyond her. She had halted at the door to the Roberts stateroom, in a long cloak, and was fumbling in the lock with a key.

Greenleaf pressed him back against the wall. "Hold it here. Let them take her."

Slocum watched her turn the key and push the stateroom door open. She'd just moved to step inside when three men sprinted around that corner in the companionway, hitting her from the rear and shoving her on through the door.

"Now," Greenleaf said, and they ran.

They plunged into the dark of the stateroom, into a confusion of sounds—stifled cries, someone wrestling on the floor, a hurried voice from somewhere across the room. Slocum put his back to the wall just inside, trying to see, not wanting to tangle with somebody on his side. He heard Roberts's startled voice straight ahead of him and Grubb saying, "Greenleaf? Slocum? You in here?"

Greenleaf's voice came from the other side of the door: "Right here."

"There's a lamp on a table behind me," Grubb said. "I can't move. I got a gun to his head, and I can't move without losing him. It's to my right. Just behind me and to my right."

"I'll get it," Slocum said.

He moved quickly and cautiously through the dark, bumped into the bed, and moved around it, reaching with one hand till he touched Grubb's back. He eased past him till he found the table and the shape of a lamp. He lit a match and lifted the chimney and touched the flame to the wick, then lifted the lamp above his head and turned.

Roberts was sitting up in bed in a nightshirt, looking wide-eyed. Grubb had one hand on the man's shoulder; the other hand held a gun to his head. Laura Roberts was on the floor, still struggling against the grip of the man who held her. The man lay on the floor behind her, both legs locked around hers, holding her arms pressed tight to her ribs. A second man had a cloth stuffed in her mouth and was fighting to tie it in place with another before she could jerk her head free. She was glaring at Slocum above the gag, and angry, strangled cries were coming through the cloth.

Grubb nudged Roberts with the pistol. "Get up. Never mind about your wife; she ain't going to be hurt. Just get up and put something on. We're going for a little walk on deck."

"What do you want? What do you want?" Roberts was blinking like a half-wit, too startled to comprehend what was happening. "You want valuables? We have no valuables here. Everything's in the purser's safe."

"We don't want your stickpins," Greenleaf said, "or your wife's bracelets. We want your boat. Now get up."

Roberts was on the side of the bed now, fumbling for his slippers. He was still half asleep, still dazed, and there was something almost childishly puzzled in his voice. "My boat? The *Gulf Queen?* But you can't steal a ship! What can you do with the *Gulf Queen?*"

"We just want to borrow it for a while," Slocum said. "Get up and get some clothes on." To Grubb he said, "They in the engine room already?"

"Wilson should have bolted for the engine room soon as he seen us jump the woman there. He had every other man with him. I can't see why he wouldn't have pulled it off. We'll know in a minute. Let's get this man moving."

They left one man to watch Laura Roberts and took her husband as he was, in a nightshirt, robe, and slippers, and headed out along the companionway toward the deck. Grubb was in the lead, Greenleaf brought up the rear. Slocum stayed behind Roberts, keeping his Colt in the old man's back, prodding him along. The old man seemed finally to come all the way awake in the cool of the wind on deck, but one look at that Colt kept him quiet. They were nearing the companionway down into the engine room—Slocum could hear the pounding of the engines above the thrashing of the paddlewheels—and now he heard footsteps vaulting toward them up the stairs of that companionway. He grabbed Roberts around the throat and put the gun to his ear, but it was one of the deckhands, coming out on deck with an old muzzle-loading pistol in his hand.

"We got the engine crew," he said, sounding a little breathless. "Had to club the chief engineer over the head, but they're in hand."

"Tell Wilson to keep those engines going," Grubb said. "And ignore any commands from the pilot house that don't come from us. We'll let you know when we got things under control."

The ship was holding fairly steady, only a faint swell rocking her from left to right. Up on the top deck Slocum could see the sea stretching away to the distant horizon, a strange flickering gray in the moonlight. Far off to starboard he saw the thin line of the Texas coast. Strange to think that a few days ago he'd been driving cattle a hundred or so miles inland from that line.

Now they were close enough to the pilot house to see two shadowy men in the dim glow of light within. Greenleaf had moved ahead. He patted the air with the flat of his hand and they all crouched down. "All right," he said, "we're going to go up there like we're on a little errand. The ship's owner and some of the crew. Roberts, you just keep quiet and look official. Otherwise you'll be too dead to care whether you get your boat back. Slocum, first thing when we get into that pilot house, you put that gun up against his head where they can see it. That ought to quiet them." He drew his big Navy Colt from its holster. "If everybody's ready, let's go do it."

The sound of the wind and the paddlewheels kept their footfalls quiet. Slocum had the Colt poised, ready to club Roberts if he tried something. They were nearing the pilothouse now. He could see the two men inside bending over what looked to be a map table. Then Greenleaf was at the door and sliding it open, and the captain was turning to look into the massive bore of Greenleaf's Colt.

The captain looked too stunned to move, but the other man sprang for a speaking tube hooked to a bracket on the wall. Grubb intercepted him, putting his own pistol up under the man's nose.

"No sense doing that. We already got the engine room. We're taking over the boat. Just relax and won't nobody get hurt."

Slocum saw the captain's eyes dart to a drawer under the map table, but if it was a pistol he wanted to go for, he thought better of it. Roberts was shaking now, like maybe that balmy night air was too much for him, but he made no move to resist.

Now Greenleaf reached for that speaking tube. To Grubb he said, "What's the name of your man in the engine room?"

"Wilson. Sam Wilson."

Greenleaf put the speaking tube to his mouth. "Wilson? Wilson, can you hear me? This is Greenleaf, in the pilothouse. We've taken over the ship. We've got the wheel."

Slocum heard a gargled reply from the speaking tube.

"Time to get the rest of the crew," Greenleaf said. "Take as many men as you can spare from the engine room and wake the crew that's off duty. Let 'em know Roberts is a hostage. Search their quarters for weapons and put a guard on them. Then do the same with the passengers. Wake up one cabin at a time. Then pick the biggest stateroom and lock them all in there."

When that gargled reply came through the speaking tube again, he hung it back in its bracket on the wall and turned his Colt on the captain again. "The *Gulf Queen's* just changed hands, Captain. From now on you take orders from us. No more scheduled stops. We'll make an unscheduled one tomorrow—pick out a nice, empty stretch of coast and put most of your people ashore—but other than that it's straight sailing for Corpus Christi. Do as you're told, and you'll get there alive."

7

Lewis heard the sound of the sea shortly after midnight.

He and Brown were out ahead of the wagons, the horses wending their slow way through the dark. Only the lighter patches of sandy ground showed a path through the sawgrass and palmetto trees. Lewis reined the cavalry mount up and Brown pulled to a halt in the dark beside him.

"You hear that?" Lewis said.

"Surf," Brown said.

"Just ahead somewhere. Maybe a hundred yards. Tell them to hold it up back there. And bring me that lantern and the pole."

Brown turned his horse and faded back into the dark. Lewis heard a murmur of voices, and then the slow rumble of wagon wheels ceased and there was only the blowing of one of the mules, the restless stirring of his own horse, the faint wash of the surf up ahead.

He calculated they were three or four miles north of Corpus Christi. If he was lucky, they should be dead even with the cove Greenleaf had agreed to shelter the boat in. He could only hope he had aimed right, and that Slocum and Greenleaf had managed to seize a vessel large enough to make the run to Vera Cruz. If the boat hadn't arrived, he would have to hide the wagons and hole up somewhere here along the coast. And the longer the wait, the more time that cavalry detachment would have to reach help.

Brown returned out of the dark, carrying a long pole they'd cut from a tree as they'd neared the coast. A lantern dangled from a saddle string back of his cantle. "I told them to hold the wagons here till we get back. Johnson's putting guards out just in case."

"That scout we sent into Corpus Christi back yet?"

"No, sir. No sign of him."

"Well, we'll just have to hope he finds us. Let's go take a look at that ocean."

Lewis sent his mount on ahead, following those patches of sandy ground. They led him through a stand of palmettos, across a flat stretch of scrub brush, and into more trees. He ducked under a limb and felt the ground begin to rise beneath him, and soon he was out in the open, mounting the gradual rise of a little dune. He could smell the sea now and the rank aroma of coastal vegetation. The sound of the surf was growing louder. Then he crested the dune and started down through the sand, feeling a faint damp wind on his face, and now out ahead of him he could see the blacker darkness which was the Gulf of Mexico, reaching out into the vast night toward the Atlantic and Africa.

He dismounted on a narrow strip of beach curving in a wide arc to the north and south. Brown dismounted beside him and took the reins of both horses. Lewis cupped a hand to his ear and listened.

Nothing except the surf and the vague noises of his horse mouthing its bit. And no sign of any boat out on the black water.

"Give me the lantern," he said.

He knelt on the sand with the lantern and pressed the lever that raised the glass from around the wick. The first match went out. He put his back to the wind and lit another, and this time the wick caught and a circle of bright light widened and steadied around him. He slung the lantern by its handle in the forks of the stick and raised it over his head, waving it slowly back and forth.

A long minute passed, then another. After what seemed ten minutes at least, he lowered the pole. Gnats already swarmed around the lantern, but nothing had altered the blackness of that water stretching away offshore.

One of the horses tossed its head, bridle chains jingling. Behind him, he sensed Brown stifling the impulse to voice what he himself was afraid of: that something had gone wrong, that Slocum and Greenleaf hadn't succeeded in hijacking a boat, or that they'd been caught by U.S. vessels after they had. Right now the most essential part of this operation could be docked under federal guard in some port between here and New Orleans.

"Maybe they just haven't got here yet," Brown said. "Maybe they laid up in the wrong place."

"There's been enough time. Greenleaf knows this area. If they got a boat, they should be here."

He was about to raise the pole again when Brown said, "Look. There it is."

Now Lewis saw it, too: the slow, swinging arc of a lantern like his own, far out on the water.

"Thank God," he said, and waved the pole high over his head.

There was an answering wave or two out on the water, then the lantern out there was lowered and abruptly went out. Lewis heard the belching of a steam engine firing up. He lowered the pole and blew his own lantern out.

"Let's move," he said. "They'll wait for us to signal from the pier, but we can't let them wait long. There might be a revenue cutter in the harbor."

Brown tied the lantern to his saddle string while Lewis mounted up again. As they started back up over the dune, he heard paddlewheels begin slowly thrashing the water out in the darkness.

Back beyond the dunes, they turned the wagons south and headed across the flat coastline toward town. Lewis felt again that eagerness that had come over him just before they'd hit the detachment in the arroyo: a sense of being useful again, engaged in what he was bred and trained for. It sharpened his senses; the creak of wheel hubs and the rattle of trace chains was suddenly louder, the salt smell of the sea suddenly stronger in the night air.

They sighted the first buildings at the edge of town after an hour's slow travel. Lewis figured it was close to two in the morning; only a few lights were showing. Then they hit a road, and the rumble of the wagon wheels grew louder, unmuffled now by grass and sand.

They passed the first dark house, and then another, and soon they were in the town itself. He had no idea where they were, only that the sea was off to the left somewhere.

"Where's that scout? What's his name?"

"I sent Hodges, sir. He's back behind the wagons, I think."

"Bring him up here. I want to talk to him."

Lewis halted the wagons. From the few lights showing, not everybody in town was asleep. The men were all wearing army uniforms, and he had Captain Jones's papers; they should be able to talk their way through any trouble, but he didn't want to take unnecessary chances. After a while, Brown returned out of the dark with Hodges, their horses moving slowly and shadowy in the dark.

"You reconnoitered the town," Lewis said to Hodges. "Where are we? Where's the pier we're aiming for?"

"We're on the main street now," Hodges said. "That light up there on the left's the constable's office and the jail. They had three officers there when I scouted it earlier."

"Any way we can get where we're going without passing it?"

"Take the next left. That'll lead us to the street along the waterfront. Then we turn right."

"All right," Lewis said. "You stay up here and lead the way."

He had Brown pass the word back, and the wagons started again. At the first corner they turned onto the street leading left toward the waterfront. They were passing between dark and shuttered buildings now, with no lights showing anywhere. A pack of dogs sidled out of an alley and crossed the street in front of them, causing Hodges' horse to shy, but that was the only sign of life. Then the street ended; the shadowy bulk of what looked to be a warehouse loomed dead ahead, and another dark street stretched away to the left and right.

"Here's where we turn," Hodges said. "Pier's about four blocks to the right."

Lewis signalled the turn, and the wagons followed him onto the dark street leading right. More warehouses loomed dark and large on his left, and he could sense the sea just beyond them. "What's it like on the pier?" he said. "Anything we got to worry about there?"

"One night watchman in a shack," Hodges said. "Lots of freight stacked on the pier. He's evidently there to keep an eye on that."

"You think he'll buy that letter from Sheridan?" Brown said.

"Not for what we'll be doing, loading army weapons onto a civilian boat in the dead of night," Lewis said. "We'll have to put him out of action before we bring the boat in."

"You want me to round up a detachment for that?"

"The three of us will do it."

"You think that's wise, sir? You being involved like that?"

"Like I said, Lieutenant, this isn't the army. Chain of command doesn't count here. These men have less invested in this operation than I have. It's only right that I take the risks."

Brown didn't say anything, but Lewis could tell he didn't like the decision. Fortunately, there was still enough army discipline in Brown to make him go along, whether chain of command mattered or not.

The truth was, Lewis thought, he was looking forward to dealing with the night watchman. It fired his blood, made him feel like a soldier again.

They had travelled a good two blocks up the street now. Lewis could see it widening out up ahead, and the end of a pier jutting left out over the water just about where the street widened. At the near edge of that pier was a narrow shack with one lit window showing.

"That's the night watchman's shack," Hodges said. "Entry's on the other side, out onto the pier. Got a two-part door, divided across the middle. There's another window, looking east toward the end of the pier. He was inside, with the top part of the door open, when I come by here."

Lewis halted the wagons and gave word they were to hold up till the night watchman was taken care of. Then he and Brown and Hodges left their horses and set off afoot toward the pier. Hodges drew a long-barrelled Colt and led the way along the front of a dark warehouse. Lewis figured the constables' office was three blocks to the right and maybe two blocks behind them. Pretty close if any shooting started. He couldn't afford to have any shooting start. If they got caught here, all hope of helping Maximilian was lost.

He had drawn his own pistol now. He was right behind Hodges. Brown was just a vague shadow behind him. Hodges halted at the corner of the warehouse, looked around it, then waved them on. They passed another, smaller building, also dark, and when they halted at the far corner of that one, Lewis could see the water off to the left and the long pier jutting out into it from the street-edge up ahead. The watchman's shack stood just where the pier met the bank.

There was no sign of the boat; he figured Slocum and Greenleaf had wisely stopped the engines somewhere out there till they saw the signal saying it was safe to come on in.

"What's beyond the pier?"

"More warehouses," Hodges said. "All dark."

"That the only night watchman?"

"Only one I saw."

The shack sat far enough out on the pier to leave a walkway all the way round it, just about wide enough for a man on the near side. Through the little window Lewis saw the top of the night watchman's head. He looked to have his head down, like maybe he was reading something. From under the pier came the quiet lap and wash of the water against the pilings.

"Let's put ourselves on three sides of him," Lewis said. "Brown, you go around where you can see in that east window. When you're sure he's alone and there's nobody else on the pier, give a wave. Hodges, you creep up under this window here. I'll go around front. When I've been there a minute or so, reach up and smash those windows. When his head's turned I'll rush him through the door."

"Sir, I think one of us should take the door," Brown said. "The commander doesn't go in before his troops."

"Just do what I tell you," Lewis said. "Watch to see when I'm in position, then signal to Hodges. Then both of you smash those windows."

Brown left them then, moving carefully out along the edge of the pier. He ducked to pass under the near window and slipped around the back corner. After a minute he reappeared, waved, and ducked back into the dark.

Lewis tapped Hodges on the arm. "Now you."

He watched till Hodges had settled himself under the near window. Then he moved out onto the pier, circled around the shack, and crept up under the door.

The top half of the door was open. Lamplight from inside revealed stacks of cargo along the opposite side of the pier. Brown's face appeared at the corner, then disappeared again. Lewis braced himself on one knee, his pistol out, his other hand on the bottom half of the door.

He waited five seconds. Ten. When he heard the sudden sound of smashing glass, he slammed the door open and burst inside.

The night watchman had wheeled toward the windows and was coming up out of his chair. At the sound of the door, he began to turn, his pistol coming out. Still in mid-stride, Lewis caught him halfway around and brought his own pistol down hard.

The man dropped as if dead. His pistol hit the chair and clattered into a corner. Lewis dropped to one knee beside him, breathing hard, harder then he'd expected; it didn't take much action anymore to get his blood pumping. He holstered his pistol, hearing running footsteps on the planks outside. He was feeling the man's pulse when Brown appeared in the doorway, Hodges right behind him.

"Everything's fine," Lewis said. "He'll live. Hodges, bring the wagons up. Brown, take this lantern and go signal off the end of the pier. Greenleaf ought to have that boat within sighting distance."

Brown took the lantern and went out, and Lewis returned the night watchman's pistol to its holster. Working in the dark now, he lifted the man back into his chair and laid his head down on his desk. Anybody looking in would see a man asleep. He made himself kneel beside the chair till the rushing of his blood had ceased, thinking maybe he was a little too old for this kind of thing. Then he got up and went back outside.

Hodges had brought the wagons up. Two lanterns slung from pylons poured light on the street at the water's edge, and the first of the wagons was being backed onto the pier. Brown was returning to the shack, the night watchman's lantern swinging, still lit at his side. Lewis could hear the slow thrashing of the paddlewheels as the boat approached, moving without lights.

"Hang the lantern where it was," he said. "Then lend a hand with those weapons crates."

He went out to the end of the pier. He could see the boat now, its huge hull looming out of the dark. The engines had stopped. The boat was drifting half-sideways toward him, eerily silent except for a tiny ripple of water at the bow. He saw Slocum and Greenleaf on the lower deck and two men with landlines at either end of the rail. Then the boat hit with a crunch and the landlines sailed out to snare the bollards rising up from the end of the dock.

When the boat was snubbed up tight, Lewis mounted the gangplank to the deck and shook hands with Slocum and Greenleaf. "Congratulations, gentlemen. You're right on time with a fine-looking boat."

"Hadn't been in that cove more than an hour when you showed up," Greenleaf said. "And the boat's brand new. Carrying the owner and his wife and some fancy passengers on her maiden voyage. We put them and half the crew ashore where they can't cause trouble. How about you? You have any trouble?"

"Didn't fire a shot. Had to club the night watchman

in that shack, but other than that things went smooth as silk."

He turned to watch the men feverishly unloading the weapons crates. Brown had returned the lantern to the night watchman's shack and was supervising the unloading. Three of the wagons had been backed onto the pier, and the fourth was waiting its turn out on the street. One crate was already being carried up the gangplank.

"Four wagonloads of Sheridan's Henry repeaters," Lewis said. "You got room for them all?"

"Lots of room," Slocum said. "Boat's carrying a cargo of lumber in the hold, but we dumped some of that overboard."

"Everything's fine then. That night watchman didn't see who hit him. Those arms shipments were secret, so neither the wagons nor the mules have U.S. markings. Time they're traced, we'll be in Mexican waters. We'll tie up with the men Bradley's training outside Vera Cruz and go on to Mexico City. Within days we should be fighting alongside Maximilian in Queretaro."

8

They arrived in the waters off Vera Cruz shortly after dawn of a foggy morning. Slocum was at the starboard rail with Lewis when they began a slow pass across the mouth of the harbor, Lewis trying with a pair of field glasses to see through the fog. The boat was barely moving. The bow rose and fell in the long swells, the paddlewheels quietly thrashing the water. Lewis had sighted two tall-masted ships farther offshore as they'd approached, and though he hadn't been able to make out the flag, they were taking no chances.

Lewis had his elbows propped on the rail; without taking the glasses from his eyes, he said, "We're close enough. Pass the word to stop the engines."

Slocum had placed a man with a rifle every few yards along the rail, just in case. Now he sent one of them up to the pilothouse, where Grubb was standing watch on the captain. Soon the slow thrashing of the paddlewheels ceased. The boat drifted, silent as a ghost, while Lewis probed the fog with his glasses.

After a while he lowered the glasses, still gazing toward shore. The air was so damp he had moisture forming in his beard. He didn't look happy.

"Something wrong?" Slocum said.

"The town's flying the Liberal flag. I can see Juarista troops in the streets. We can't land here."

Slocum took the glasses. The sun rising behind him was beginning to burn off some of the fog. It was already getting hot. He scanned the long swells in toward shore, saw the remains of a schooner wrecked on a coral reef, a graveyard on a little harbor island, then the first row of whitewashed, flat-roofed buildings, a street running up from the docks, coconut palms, the high walls of a fort, more streets, more buildings: Vera Cruz. The fort was flying some kind of flag but he couldn't make it out.

"You think we're too late? You think Maximilian's already lost his war?"

"Not necessarily." Lewis took the glasses back, wiped the lenses. "Juarez already controlled several large towns when we left for the States. With the French gone, he'd have taken this port soon as he could. That doesn't mean Maximilian's not still in command in Queretaro."

The fog was burning off to seaward, exposing the long blue line of the horizon. Slocum gazed back past the stern, toward where they'd seen those ships. Not even the masts were in sight. "How much trouble's this give us? There must be some place along here we can put ashore."

"I was counting on shipping those rifles inland by railroad," Lewis said. "Pick up Bradley where he's headquartered and go on to Mexico City. I have contacts there, Princess Salm-Salm and Colonel Graham. Can't do it that way now. Got to contact Bradley first, have him bring some pack animals here. We'll have to go the whole way by horse or mule."

"Where's Bradley located?"

"He took over an abandoned hacienda near Paso del Sol. About thirty miles inland, if he's still there. Could be the Juaristas have driven him out."

The decks groaned as the boat rocked slowly on the swells. Slocum became aware of the men watching him from along the rail. "Well, there's only one way to find out. Somebody's going to have to go look him up, and thirty miles is a long hike. I'll go have a word with our captain. See if we can put ashore somewhere farther down the coast."

Two hours later the boat was laid up at anchor in a tree-lined cove south of Vera Cruz. The fog had burned off the water. The sun was up high and hot in the blue sky overhead, but the air was too damp and muggy to be pleasant. Slocum had two of Grubb's sailors rigging up lines to lower a dinghy over the side near the stern, and Hodges and Brown were standing by to row the dinghy to shore. Slocum, a bedroll and a rifle slung over his shoulder, was scanning the dense green growth beyond the beach and thinking of the long hike to wherever this Lee Bradley was. He wasn't looking forward to the walk.

Now Lewis came back out on deck, carrying a shoulder bag and one of the Henry repeaters. He came to the rail, where Hodges was climbing into the dinghy, and glanced up at the sun. "Let's get this thing in the water. We've got a long walk ahead of us, and we don't want to do any more of it in the dark than we have to."

"Hope you can find your way there in the dark," Slocum said.

"I believe so," Lewis said. "We'll find an old roadbed the other side of Vera Cruz. Once we're on that we're all right as long as we watch out for Juaristas."

Greenleaf had come up from the engine room to see them off. Now the sailors started lowering the dinghy over the side, Hodges clinging to the gunwales. Slocum watched it hit the water and begin to rise and heave on the little swells rolling in toward the beach. Hodges had an oar up, using it to hold himself away from the hull of the boat. Now Brown climbed over the rail, lowered himself hand over hand down the rope into the dinghy, and took up the second oar. Lewis handed Slocum his pack and rifle and took the rope Brown had just relinquished.

Greenleaf was holding to one of the ropes fixed to the dinghy. "When can we expect you back?"

"May be a few days," Lewis said. "We'll have to round up enough animals to carry both men and weapons all the way to Queretaro. You'll have to expect us when you see us."

"We may not be here when you get back," Greenleaf said. "We're too close to Vera Cruz. I figure I'll pull the boat out and sit offshore maybe a mile. Even then we might have to weigh anchor if some passing ship gets suspicious of us. We'd better figure some way to rendezvous."

Lewis gazed off toward the beach, thinking. "Give us four days. After that you better bring the boat in here looking for us at least twice a day. We can wait that long for you. Make it dawn and dusk, so we'll know when to look for you." Then he took his pack and rifle back from Slocum, slung them over his shoulder, and went down the rope into the dinghy.

"Keep an eye on him," Greenleaf said. "He keeps forgetting he's not a young man anymore."

"I'll do that." Slocum got a leg up over the rail and grabbed on to the rope. "And don't forget to come in here looking for us. I don't want to get stuck on this beach with a bunch of Mexican bandits."

Then he went down the side after Lewis.

It was after midnight when they neared the hacienda Lewis said Bradley was holed up in. By that time Slocum had blisters on both heels and was as near to beat as he'd been any time since the War. He couldn't remember ever seeing sorrier country: sandy and bleak near the coast, with nothing but scorched and stunted bushes and here and there a cactus; and then miles of dank, suffocating marshland, empty save for occasional wild cattle knee-deep in the marshes, providing a perch for birds pecking bugs off the hide of their backs. Slocum was sweltering. His clothes, sweated through, had been clinging to his skin for hours. He'd been glad to see night come on, hoping things would cool off, but the air just seemed to get wetter and steamier and harder to breathe, and the very undergrowth along the trail seemed to give off heat, and the night air seemed to blow back in his face like a giant bellows till the heat and the dampness and the discomfort even stopped him worrying about Juaristas. Lewis said this marshy coastal strip was notorious for diseases like yellow fever, and they hadn't seen anybody since early afternoon anyway, Juarista or otherwise.

Lewis had matched him stride for stride despite those short legs. Now as the ground began to rise he seemed even to quicken his pace, as if sensing they were close and wanting to get on with it, to get those men and weapons inland where they could do some good to that Emperor he had replaced the South with as something to believe in and be attached to. There was a bit of a moon, and Slocum could see they were passing through large over-arching trees draped with some kind of vines. The trail had narrowed till the two of them could barely walk side by side. Every now and then one of those vines, unseen in the dark, would brush past his face like a snake, causing him to start and bat the air. Then it too would pass, and there would be Lewis in front of him, never slowing, leading him on.

Now he began hearing something strange up ahead, something out of place, something he couldn't quite identify. Lewis started to slow, and he knew Lewis had heard it too. The trail wound on another hundred yards or so, and then he began to see a glow of light through the undergrowth up ahead, and now he realized with surprise that what he'd been hearing was music. Mariachi music. Somewhere up ahead was a mariachi band, trumpets loud and clear on the night air.

Lewis had stopped on the trail. Slocum could just make out his face and the gray of his beard in the moonlight. He had his head cocked to one side, listening.

"That can't be Bradley," he said.

"Is that where the hacienda ought to be?"

"That's the hacienda. I recognize the terrain here, but that can't be Major Bradley. The Juaristas may rarely make it up here, but Major Bradley would have better security than that."

"Maybe you were right the first time. Maybe the Juaristas drove him out. Maybe somebody else took over the hacienda. Whoever it is, sounds like they're having themselves a fiesta."

Now the music stopped. In its place Slocum could hear the continuous murmuring of a crowd having a good time. He heard a woman's laugh rise up above the rest, and then the music started up again, bright and festive. Whoever it was was definitely having a party.

"Let's get closer," Lewis said. "I want to see what's going on. If it looks right, we might risk going in and asking after Bradley. Somebody ought to know what's happened to him."

Slocum slipped the Henry repeater off his shoulder and levered a round into the chamber. When Lewis had done the same, they started on. The music grew louder and the light closer. Slocum began to glimpse a building through the trees, lamplight pouring out windows along what looked to be a terrace at the back of it. The trail bent around some undergrowth and opened out onto clear ground. Now the building was dead ahead of them, a sprawling stone structure with high tiled roofs and a waterless fountain growing moss on a brick terrace visible in the light from the windows. They were still a good fifty yards away, but Slocum could see people moving around inside.

Then from the brush to the right of the trail came a man's voice: *"Alto. Quien va?"*

Slocum grabbed Lewis by the arm, but Lewis had already frozen in his tracks. Now he heard movement in the brush on his left and the quiet *snick-snick* of the hammer being cocked on a pistol. "You're the one knows Mexican," he said. "You better start speaking it."

The first sentry had stepped out into the light, a swarthy Mexican holding a brace of pistols levelled at them about belly-height. *"Quien va?"* he repeated.

Lewis said something in Spanish, something with the name Bradley in it. The sentry took a closer look at him then and glanced toward the house. Slocum found himself hoping Bradley was a lot looser in his security than Lewis wanted to believe. He would accept loose security if it meant these were Bradley's men.

The second one had stepped out from the brush on the left now, a rough-looking gent with a bushy moustache and a mouth full of teeth big enough for a horse. He and the first one were trading some rapid talk, with Lewis getting an occasional word in. The one with the moustache waggled a rifle now and said something Slocum knew was meant for him.

"What's he saying? Did he say Bradley's in there?"

Lewis didn't take his eyes off the sentries. "Claims he doesn't know anybody named Bradley. Wants us to disarm ourselves. One at a time. I told him you'd go first."

The music was still coming loud and festive from the house. Slocum eyed the sentries and eased out into the light a little farther. Carefully he laid his rifle on the ground, unbuckled his gunbelt, and laid that down, too. He had barely stepped back beside Lewis when the sentry with the moustache had that Henry repeater in his hands, jabbering in Mexican to the other one.

Without turning his head, Slocum said, "He likes the repeater. Let's hope he likes us. You get anything about Bradley yet?"

"No." Lewis was laying his weapons on the ground. "Only thing I got so far was that these fellows don't like Juaristas any more than we do."

"That's something, anyway."

Slocum felt a rifle barrel prod his back; the first sentry was behind them now, herding them up toward the house. The one with the moustache was carrying their weapons, fiddling with the lever action on one of the Henrys. Slocum hoped he didn't accidentally fire the thing; in a situation like this, one shot could set off a disaster. He still had a knife in his boot scabbard, where the sentries hadn't looked, but a knife wouldn't do him much good against armed bandits.

Now they were halted at the edge of the terrace, and the first sentry went on ahead, toward a door standing open into what looked to be one end of the room the crowd was in. Slocum saw the quick flash of a woman passing the door: white blouse, brown arms, black hair. The first sentry stopped near an open window and shouted something at somebody inside.

The mariachi music stopped. In the sudden silence Slocum heard the same woman's laugh he'd heard before, loud and drunken, and then the voice of a man cutting her short. The sentry beside him stirred, shifted from foot to foot, his breathing harsh and loud. Slocum could smell him, the sweat of a man who took one bath a year, who smoked strong tobacco and ate too much spicy food.

Now a man appeared in the doorway, silhouetted

against the light, a big man casually carrying a long-barrelled pistol in one dangling hand.

"Que pasa?"

The first sentry said something in Spanish, and the big man came out onto the terrace, walking with the unsteady gait of a man who had had too much to drink. Slocum felt a rifle barrel in the small of his back; he and Lewis were nudged forward into the light, and now he got a better look at the man with the pistol. He was taller than Slocum and broad-shouldered, a huge moustache hiding his mouth, a gold-embroidered black sombrero slung down his back.

Now Lewis said, "Major Bradley, I would appreciate your calling these men off."

"Lewis?" the man said. "That you, Lewis?"

"Major Bradley, if this were the regular army I can assure you you'd be facing a court-martial. I left you charged with organizing a force to fight for the Emperor. I didn't expect to find you organizing drunken brawls instead."

"Ah, Colonel," the man said, "you turned up after all. Thought you'd settled down in Texas or somewhere. Maybe got yourself killed. Hold on a minute while I take myself a leak, and we'll go inside and talk."

Bradley stuck the pistol in his waistband, ambled over to the side of the terrace, and started fumbling with his pants. Slocum had trouble picturing the man as a Confederate major; with his sun-darkened skin, the huge moustache, and the clothes he was wearing, he looked as Mexican as any of his men. He was standing spraddle-legged at the edge of the terrace, splattering the bricks between his feet. Slocum could sense Lewis getting angrier beside him.

"Major Bradley," Lewis said, "I'd appreciate a civil word when you're finished."

Bradley finished and buttoned up. "Come on in, Colonel." He hitched his pants up and waved them toward the door. "Bring your friend with you."

A burst of Spanish brought the sentry over to give Slocum and Lewis their weapons back. Slocum was still buckling his gunbelt on as he followed Bradley inside.

The crowd had fallen silent. The air was full of smoke. There looked to be a good two dozen men around the room, sitting or lying on pallets near the walls, most with a woman and a bottle. Half of them wore bandoliers crossed over their chests, and every man had a muzzle-loader leaning up against the wall beside him. Here and there Slocum saw female eyes flashing at him above a pair of bare shoulders. Lewis, threading his way through the crowd behind Bradley, looked to be working hard at keeping himself under control, but Slocum was paying more attention to the unfriendly eyes examining him from every side.

Then Bradley took a seat in a big leather chair mounted like a throne on a dais at the near end of the room and waved them to a leather settee at right angles to him.

"Let me get you a drink, gentlemen."

He snapped his fingers, and down at the other end of the room the mariachi band began playing again. A sultry, shapely señorita brought him a drink and perched herself on the arm of his chair, and a younger but no less shapely girl brought drinks for Lewis and Slocum and sat on the settee between them.

Bradley raised his glass and grinned. "Welcome

back to Mexico, Colonel. Things aren't quite the same as when you left."

"I can see that," Lewis said. "I'd like an explanation. Perhaps you can tell me what's going on."

"What it looks like. A party." Bradley waved his glass at the room, where the hum of talk had risen up again. "These men did good work today. They deserve a little party."

"I can see it's a party. That wasn't what I meant. I want an explanation. For one thing, I cannot understand your permitting this noise. From what I've seen, Juarez controls this part of the country. Yet here you are, light flooding out the windows, your men half drunk, women everywhere. That is hardly what I would call good security."

"Well, Colonel, you don't understand what—"

"Obviously I don't understand." Lewis was sitting ramrod-straight on the edge of the settee, his face gone pale with anger. "You were to be preparing the ground for when I returned. I've covered thousands of miles in very ltttle time, developing plans, recruiting men. I organized a force strong enough to steal an arms shipment from General Sheridan himself. We commandeered a ship out of New Orleans and brought it all way to Mexico. And now, to contact you, Slocum and I have walked all day and half the night from Vera Cruz. We expected to find a well-trained and disciplined force when we got here."

Slocum was beginning to get an idea how much this operation meant to Lewis. He could see it dawning on Bradley too. Bradley slapped his shapely señorita on the rump and said something to her, and she got up and took the younger girl away with her.

"Colonel, let me tell you something," Bradley said. "You been out of the country damned near three months. A lot's changed since then. I've been training these men, but there's no sense training them to fight as part of an army. Maximilian went and got himself surrounded by forty thousand Juaristas. Queretaro's been under siege for weeks now. What little I hear from the capital, he won't hold out much longer."

Lewis sank back on the settee, looking like the day's walk had suddenly caught up with him. "You heard that from Graham?"

"From Graham himself. He's still in Mexico City. Juarez hasn't taken it yet, he's concentrated around Queretaro, but that's the only reason he hasn't."

Slocum was counting days, wondering if this whole thing had been for nothing. "When did you hear from Graham last?"

"Who are you?" Bradley said. "What's your say in this?"

"The name's Slocum. I asked a question."

Bradley gave him a blunt once-over; whatever he saw seemed to satisfy him. "He sent a boy here about three weeks ago. Said the Imperial Army had itself surrounded. Forty thousand Juaristas against maybe a quarter that many on Maximilian's side."

Lewis looked to be recovering from the shock. He got up from the settee now and started pacing the floor. "Major, this doesn't change the situation. We've got a boatload of men and weapons off the coast of Vera Cruz. We need horses and pack mules to get them overland to Maximilian. It's your job to supply them. It's my job to decide what to do when we get there."

"Maybe if this was the regular army," Bradley said.

"It ain't. Face facts, Colonel. Those repeaters can't do Maximilian any good. You give them to me, and I'll take a pack train to the coast and help you offload them."

"No, Major. So long as the Emperor needs help, we're here to give it. This is our country now. We owe as much allegiance to Maximilian as we ever did to Jeff Davis."

"Yeah, and that was a lost cause, too. Colonel, the Juaristas are about to take this country over. I've got an understanding with them. We stick to raiding the rich, and they don't bother us. I'm not giving this up for another lost cause. Let us have those rifles, and we'll help you get whoever's left from the colony back to the States. That's the only smart thing to do now."

Shocked, Lewis stopped pacing. "Major, a soldier does not make war against his own supporters. What you're doing is treasonous."

"And you're living in a dream world, Colonel. Maximilian's as good as dead. Forget him. Give me those rifles, and I'll help you the only way I can."

"Never, Major. Never! I will scuttle that boat first."

Slocum came up off the settee to put himself between them, blocking Lewis's way, his back to Bradley. "We ain't getting anywhere this way, Colonel. Let it go. If Bradley don't want to fight Juaristas, we can't make him."

Through the blare of the mariachi band Slocum could tell the hum of talk had fallen off. The Mexicans were watching Lewis. Two or three had gotten to their feet and stood facing the dais, hands propped on their hips just above their pistol butts. Bradley's woman and the younger one were drifting back along one wall, as if to get out of the way. Lewis looked too steamed up to notice; he was standing his ground, glaring past Slocum at Bradley.

"Let it go, Colonel," Slocum said. "We don't want to bring Maximilian men that won't fight for him. And we can't afford to fight each other. Let's see what we can do. Bradley wants rifles, we want mules. Maybe we can trade. We give Bradley enough rifles for his men, and he supplies a pack train and an escort to Queretaro. Once we're there, he can drop out, but we've brought the Emperor what we can. What do you say?"

Lewis was still glaring at Bradley. Slocum waited, knowing things depended more on what Bradley said. If Bradley decided he didn't like the offer or the situation, he just might turn them over to those Juaristas he'd got so friendly with.

After a bit Bradley said, "Sounds fair. I'd say that's fair. We supply a pack train, help offload the weapons and escort you to Queretaro. How about it, Colonel?"

Lewis finally looked away. "Very well. If that's the best that can be salvaged from the situation. But I want to move quickly. I want those mules acquired and started toward the coast as soon as possible."

"Don't have to acquire mules," Bradley said. "We already got a pack train. We can head out tomorrow."

"Good," Lewis said. "And now, if you will show me to a bed, I would like to retire. We have had a long day." He wouldn't look at Bradley now, and he looked tired and drained, like maybe it was more than a day's long walk that had caught up with him. When Bradley beckoned his woman up and had her lead Lewis off toward a set of stairs visible through a corridor back of Bradley's chair, Slocum could see the man was half asleep on his feet already.

The mariachi band had flared up again, some raucous number with a lot of high trumpets in it. Slocum found Bradley watching him with a wry grin.

"I seen you watching Josefa earlier," Bradley said. "You want her?"

Slocum looked to see the girl who had been with Bradley's woman was standing just back of his left shoulder, looking down, hands clasped in front of her. He figured Bradley had it in mind to get more than his share of those rifles somewhere down the line and was trying to soften him up with the offer of a woman. But she was pretty—young and shapely, her large breasts swelling above the low cut of her gown.

He looked back to Bradley. "She yours to give?"

Bradley grinned and nodded toward the corridor. "Let's just say I have influence. She's that one's younger sister."

Bradley said something in Spanish to the girl, and she came shyly over and slipped her arm through Slocum's. At the feel of her warm flesh against his, Slocum felt something hot start up in his belly.

"She'll give you a bath," Bradley said. "If she's like her sister, she gives good baths."

Slocum looked down at the girl beside him. "I hope you know what you're getting into," he said.

"She knows," Bradley said.

The girl flashed the white of her eyes at Slocum and essayed a smile. *"No me gusta estar solo,"* she said, and took his hand and led him off down the corridor toward the stairs.

9

A faint breeze rippled the water of the cove. Overhead, the palm fronds swayed and sawed against each other. Slocum was sitting against the trunk of a coconut palm, smoking his third cigarette in an hour, watching the slow roll of the ocean far out beyond the mouth of the cove. Cool evening shadows were already inching out across the beach, but the water was still blue and flickering sunlight at him. There was no sign of the *Gulf Queen*.

"Been two hours now," Bradley said. "Where's that damned boat?"

"Take it easy," Slocum said. "It'll be here. Supposed to check in here twice a day, sunrise and sunset. It ain't sunset yet."

Bradley was propped against another tree a few feet away, idly chopping at the ground with a machete. Lewis had wandered down the beach by himself. Slocum could see him down there, standing with his legs apart and his hands behind his back, brooding out at that empty ocean. Bradley's men were holding the animals out of sight back up in the brush above the beach.

"If it ain't here by dark, I'm pulling out." Bradley got up and slipped the machete in to the sheath slung from his belt. "I'm going to post new sentries. Give a holler if that boat shows up."

"I'll do that," Slocum said.

Bradley slipped into the trees and thrashed back through the dense underbrush. Slocum watched that patch of blue ocean out there, hoping any minute to see the *Gulf Queen* heave into view. Two days had passed since he'd seen her last; anything could have gone wrong in two days. If something had, it would be Bradley he would have to rely on. By now it was clear Lewis had lived too high in the Carlota Colony and too far removed from the average Mexican to learn much of the language or to know how to deal with them. Twice on their way from Paso del Sol, two dozen men with bandoliers across their chests and a pack train of mules, they had encountered patrols of Juarista troops, and it was only Bradley's command of the language and his way with Mexicans that kept things from going wrong. Bradley knew how to offer a bribe, how to introduce the subject of money without ruffling anybody's feathers. If that boat didn't show up and Bradley left, Slocum wasn't sure he and Lewis could get out of this country.

Then he heard it coming from the south: the muffled thrashing of the paddlewheels. He saw Lewis turn and look to see if he'd heard it too and then start along the beach toward him. The boat was still beyond that greenly wooded point of land; he couldn't even see smoke from the stacks. But he recognized her sound, and he tossed the cigarette to the sand and got to his feet.

He could hear Bradley thrashing back through the underbrush. Bradley came out onto the beach, bringing one of the Mexicans with him, just as the *Gulf Queen* nosed into sight. Slocum could see the superstructure white in the sun, and the black bow knifing through the water.

"That your boat?" Bradley said.

Lewis had joined them now. "That's it," he said. "The *Gulf Queen*. Carrying a whole wagon-train load of repeating rifles and nearly two dozen men come to fight for Maximilian."

Slocum could hear the Mexicans talking back in the trees. Likely they had never seen a steamship like the *Gulf Queen* before. She had emerged from behind that clump of land at the point and was turning in toward shore. Now she began to slow, and Slocum could see she was turning all the way around and coming to a coasting stop facing back south. The last wash of sound came rolling in across the cove, followed by a sudden silence as the engines were shut down and the paddlewheels stopped beating the water.

"Something's wrong," Lewis said. "They're not coming all the way in."

The *Gulf Queen* was heaving slowly up and down on the roll of its own wake. Slocum could see a man or two along the rail, but it was too far away to make out who. Lewis took off his hat and walked down toward the water, waving the hat over his head, but Slocum figured they'd already been seen through the field glasses. Somebody was lowering the dinghy over the side. Soon two men descended ropes from the rail, climbed into the dinghy, and began rowing in toward shore.

"What's the matter?" Bradley said. "They bring the big boat all the way in before?"

"When they let us off they did," Lewis said. "Something's got to be wrong if they're laying up out there, but I can't think what it could be."

When the dinghy got close, Slocum saw Hodges at the oars, along with one of Grubb's sailors. The *Gulf Queen* was still rocking gently out at the mouth of the cove, and men were moving idly along the deck; whatever was wrong didn't look to need fixing in a hurry. Then the dinghy was nearing shore, and he and Bradley waded out into the shallow surf and seized it by the gunwales and ran it up onto the sand.

Hodges took his hat off and wiped sweat off his brow. "We got a problem. Captain says he can't bring the boat in. Says there's an underwater reef across the entrance, and the boat draws too much water to make it across."

"There can't be," Lewis said. "We brought the boat in here when you let Slocum and me off. He's got to be lying."

"He says it was high tide then. Says it's low tide now and we'll have to wait twelve hours before we can come in. Greenleaf said I should come tell you while he figures out what to do."

"We can't wait twelve hours," Bradley said. "Vera Cruz ain't more than a mile up the beach. That's a major Juarista headquarters. We can't talk our way clear if they come snooping around. Something better get straightened out soon, or I'm taking my men and my mules out of here."

Slocum figured Bradley was making idle threats; he wanted those repeaters too bad to pull out entirely now. But it wouldn't be smart to leave him alone here to hatch something up with his Mexicans.

"Colonel, you stay here with Bradley. I'll go see what's happening. Soon as we got things straight I'll send the dinghy back. Now help me get this thing in the water and turned around again."

Greenleaf was leaning on the rail when they brought the dinghy in alongside the *Gulf Queen*. The paddle-wheels were still dead in the water. A deckhand tossed a rope over the side, and Slocum grabbed it and went hand over hand up onto the deck.

"Sorry you had to come out the hard way," Greenleaf said. "I told the captain to put into that cove, and he shut the thing down on me. Just put her hard to port and shut the engines down."

"I understand he says there's a reef down there. And that he can't cross it till the tide comes up."

"There's a reef all right. I took a look over the bow and saw it. You'd been looking, you could have seen it from the dinghy. Not more than four or five feet underwater. We'd have found it sooner, but I've been just putting the dinghy in to see if you were there. Didn't want to take this big boat in every day. Draw too much attention if somebody's watching."

"You think he's telling the truth about having to wait twelve hours?"

"Don't know. Let's go up to the pilothouse. I sent somebody to get Grubb out of bed. He's been going without sleep keeping that engine crew honest, but he knows about this sort of thing. Maybe he can figure out what's what."

Grubb was already in the pilothouse, rummaging

around in what Slocum had by now learned to call a storage locker. One of Lewis's men was leaning against the forward bulkhead, a pistol in his belt, standing watch on the captain, who had his back to a corner, arms folded, brow furrowed, bristling defiance through his gray beard.

"There's no need to look," the captain was saying. "You'll just find what I've told you. Your Mister Greenleaf here saw the reef for himself."

"I know," Grubb said. "You told me already." He hauled out a sheaf of maps and started shuffling through them. "There should be charts for this area in here. Maybe we can find something on them."

"What's this about waiting twelve hours?" Slocum said. "How do you know that?"

The captain shrugged and nodded toward Grubb. "He'll find it. It's on the charts."

"We can't afford to wait twelve hours," Slocum protested.

"You'll have to. There's no choice," the captain replied.

Grubb had pulled one chart out and set the others aside. "He's right about the reef. Here's the cove we're at, and you can see the reef marked." He was running his finger down a list of numbers on the side of the map. "Afraid he's right about the time, too. High tide at Vera Cruz is five-fifty in the morning. That's just about the time we first put in here. Low tide's at six-fourteen. About what it is now."

The captain allowed himself a smirk. "Told you you'd have to wait."

Slocum figured he was hoping some passing ship would take an interest in them and pull alongside. Or maybe he had some plot hatching amongst his officers and crew, something about to come to a head. The captain of an ocean-going vessel likely wouldn't let his ship be hijacked without trying to do something about it.

Grubb was still scanning the charts. "Wait a minute. Here's a cove not two miles down the coast. There's no reef in it, according to this. We should be able to get in there."

"How about it?" Slocum said. "Can you take us close enough in toward shore to offload?"

The captain came reluctantly over to look at the chart. "Not sure. Could be too shallow. That chart's not accurate."

"Was accurate enough when you *wanted* to prove something by it," Slocum said. "We're going in that cove. Grubb, make a drawing of that stretch of coast and have Hodges take it to Bradley. Bradley'll need some way of finding where we're headed. Captain, soon as that dinghy's back aboard, we're going to fire up your engines. Then we'll see how accurate your chart is."

The sun had set by the time the last load of crated rifles was ashore. Despite much loud worrying by the captain, the *Gulf Queen* had made it into the new cove with no difficulty. They had dropped anchor about a hundred yards off the narrow curve of beach and used the cargo hoists to lower the crates into lifeboats to be rowed ashore. The captain was slumped now sullenly in a corner of the pilothouse, going over the charts for the waters north of Vera Cruz. From his perch on the storage locker Slocum was watching Bradley's men splash out into the water to guide the last of the boats up onto the sand.

Lewis had come back aboard and was standing on

deck just aft of the pilothouse with a pair of field glasses, looking out to sea. "There are ships out there," he said. "Those same two ships we saw through the fog when we got here. They're moving south under sail."

"They been patrolling off Vera Cruz the whole time we were gone," Slocum said. "Greenleaf saw them, but he said they never bothered the *Gulf Queen*."

The train of pack mules was lined along the pale sand, barely visible against the dark backdrop of trees. Bradley's men had the lifeboat beached and were breaking open the crates and transferring the rifles to the mules' packsaddles. Slocum checked the sky to see how much longer the light would last. He had locked what remained of the *Gulf Queen*'s crew in the Roberts' stateroom and sent everybody ashore except Greenleaf, who was making a last search through the boat. When that was done, they could leave.

Lewis still had the field glasses up to his eyes. "They're flying the Austrian flag. Could be a good sign. Maybe it means Austria's going to come in and help Maximilian. After all, his brother's the Austrian Emperor. Surely his own brother would help him."

"If he is, we ought to find out. Would your contacts in Mexico City know?"

"They should. If not Graham, then Princess Salm-Salm. The Salm-Salms came to Mexico just two months before the French left—I suspect the Prince wanted a war to fight in—but they have friends in the diplomatic corps. The Prince's father rules one of the Prussian princedoms."

Greenleaf had come up the ladder and crossed to the pilothouse. "Everybody's ashore. I checked the crew's quarters for weapons and pitched what I could find overboard. Unless somebody's got some hid, they're clean."

"Good," Slocum said, and swung down off the storage locker. "Let's get off this boat."

On the beach the last of the crates had been unloaded, and Bradley's men had pushed the lifeboat back out into the water. The tail end of the pack train was just disappearing up into the trees. Bradley had led four saddle horses down onto the sand and was looking out toward the boat now.

"Time to go." Slocum took the stateroom key out of his pocket and showed it to the captain. "I'm going to leave this in the lifeboat we take ashore. You can come get it when we're gone, but don't be in any hurry. I see you before we're out of sight of this cove, I'll shoot you. Understand?"

The captain nodded. "You've nothing to worry about. I want no more trouble."

"You didn't have no trouble, just an unscheduled trip to Mexico." Slocum put the key back in his pocket and went out to join Greenleaf and Lewis. "All right, let's head for Mexico City."

10

A rooster's crow woke Slocum shortly after dawn. Dry cornhusks crackled under his blankets as he rolled up on one elbow. They had bedded down in the dark the night before; now he got a better look at the place Bradley had picked to put them in. The room was quiet save for the men snoring in their bedrolls on the floor around him. Dried corn was heaped in bins around the thick adobe walls, and several sacks of grain stood in one corner. He pulled his pants on over his longjohns, crossed to the paneless window, and lifted the straw blind aside.

Morning sunlight already warmed the dusty little plaza outside. Three chickens roosted on the rim of a well in its center, and a lean pig dozed in the shade of another adobe hut across the way. Otherwise, the village looked deserted. Bradley had been a little rough getting the locals to provide shelter, and likely they'd fled to the brush in case any Juarista troops happened through.

Bradley, Slocum knew, would have his men in one of the adobe huts across the plaza; he'd been keeping them separate ever since leaving Vera Cruz. Slocum wasn't happy about Bradley taking charge of things, but neither Brown nor Lewis spoke enough Spanish to get things done. That meant he had to follow Bradley's lead, and he didn't like being led by a man he didn't trust.

Through the door standing open at the rear of the hut he caught the smell of fresh coffee. He put the rest of his clothes on and went out to find Lewis sitting beside a little fire on the bare packed dirt of the yard, waiting for a pot of coffee to brew.

Slocum brought a tin cup from a pack leaning against the rear wall of the hut and hunkered down beside Lewis. "Brown not back yet?"

"No," Lewis said.

Slocum saw the mules picketed off in the trees back of the hut. The packs had been unloaded and heaped together and were being watched by two guards. The guards, he noted, were Bradley's men.

"Should have been back by now, don't you think?"

"I expected him back before dawn. He had time enough." Lewis peered into the coffeepot, then replaced the lid and went back to staring pensively off toward the southwest.

Slocum took the makings from his vest pocket and began rolling up a smoke. At the southwest edge of the clearing, where Lewis had his eyes fastened, he noticed another guard, also one of Bradley's Mexicans. If he remembered rightly, that was where the little mule trail into Mexico City began. Lewis had sent Brown out that trail the night before, looking for Colonel Graham, his contact from the Carlota Colony. Mexico City was supposed to be only two or three hours' ride away. Brown should definitely have been back by now.

He heard a sound behind him and turned to see Greenleaf emerging from the hut, still stiff and groggy from sleep. The other men were coming awake and stirring around inside.

"That coffee ready to drink?" Greenleaf asked.

Lewis checked the pot again, lifting it off the hot coals with a rag wrapped around the handle. "Just ready."

Now Bradley came around the corner of the hut, carrying his rifle, bandoliers already in place across his chest. He rummaged another tin cup from the pack against the back of the hut and came over to pour his own coffee. "Your man's not back yet. I think our friend Maximilian's already lost his war. I can smell it in the air. Could be Mexico City's already under Juarista rule and Brown's got himself shot."

Lewis didn't rise to the bait; he was back gazing off toward that trail. "If that's so," he said, "I expect we'll find out."

For several days Slocum had been hiding a suspicion that Bradley just might be right. Despite sticking to back-country burro trails, they'd had to dodge Juarista patrols half a dozen times on the way from Vera Cruz. If Maximilian had his whole army engaging the enemy in Queretaro, there must be a lot of enemy left over. With Bradley breaking trail, they had wound across what seemed half of Mexico, sometimes emerging out of deep jungle to cross thousands of acres once planted in cotton and coffee and now overgrown with brush, where half-hidden in the mossy trees they could see the crumbling and bullet-riddled walls of haciendas laid waste by a civil war Lewis said had been going on for half a century. Occasionally out of the jungle there would appear thatched-hut villages so primitive they might have been in Africa. The inhabitants, the only people they encountered, were stone-faced Indian peasants so removed from the world of 1867 they might more readily have known the fate of the last Incan king than that of Maximilian the First. But this village Bradley had called a halt in the night before was on the high plateau of Mexico City. Slocum could even see snow-covered mountains in the distance. If Lewis's friend Graham ever arrived, they might finally learn how things stood in Queretaro.

The rest of the men were up and squatting around an iron cook-pot on the fire eating a breakfast of tortillas and beans cooked up by one of Bradley's Mexicans when Slocum saw the sentry at the head of the trail come suddenly alert. The sentry came erect off a tree trunk he'd been leaning against and stood spraddle-legged with his back to the clearing, gazing southwest into the trees. After a moment, he moved quickly out of sight in that direction, evidently trying for a look at something he'd heard. For maybe ten seconds Slocum watched the spot where he'd entered the trees. When he didn't reappear, Slocum put his plate down and got to his feet.

"Somebody coming."

The group around the fire erupted as men hastily set their plates aside and dived for their rifles. Bradley's Mexicans scattered into the trees where the mules were picketed. Greenleaf took cover with a dozen other men behind the hut they'd spent the night in, and a half a dozen others dashed back inside. Slocum ended up sprawled in the dirt of the yard, using the cook-pot for cover, his Henry repeater trained on the mouth of the trail. From the corner of his eye he could see Hodges and another man peering over the hut's windowsill, watching the trees.

Lewis was sheltering in the doorway of the hut. "Where'd that sentry go?" he called to Slocum.

"Went back along the trail. That's what made me jump. Looked like he heard something."

"If it's a Juarista patrol, let's hope it's small. Anything bigger than a platoon and we're in trouble."

From the back corner of the hut Greenleaf said, "Quiet. I think I heard something."

Slocum put his attention back on the mouth of the trail. Now he heard something, too: the sound of horses approaching, still out of sight in the trees. Then the sentry reappeared and signalled that things were all right. Behind him came Brown, followed by a gray-bearded gent on a white horse and a young Mexican on a mule.

Slocum got to his feet and dusted himself off, and Greenleaf came up behind him leading the men who'd sheltered behind the hut. Lewis stepped out of the doorway and waved to those inside.

"It's all right," he said. "It's the lieutenant. He's brought our friend."

Bradley was bringing his Mexicans back out of the trees when the three riders reined up beside the fire. Lewis held the horse's bridle as the older man dismounted, then moved to embrace him and shake his hand.

"Been a long time, my friend. I was afraid Juarez had done you in, but here you are whole and sound. Sit and have some breakfast."

Like Lewis, Graham wore an old Confederate officer's tunic and gloves. He removed the gloves, looking around at the men gathering behind the hut. "You got this far with this many," he said. "I confess I didn't expect it. I was surprised to see the lieutenant. So much has happened since you left, I thought we'd seen the last of you."

"Took a while to gather up the men I wanted." Lewis introduced the Americans, ignoring the Mexicans crouched in a line in front of the packs of weapons and ammunition. Likely he considered them hirelings. And they didn't speak English, anyway. "We can talk while we eat. You'd better have some breakfast."

Graham settled himself on his haunches between Brown and the young Mexican he'd brought with him. "It's more in the nature of lunch for me, but I'll have some."

"You had me worried." Lewis was bending over the dying fire, pouring coffee into a cup. "When you weren't here by dawn, I was afraid the Juaristas had already taken the city."

Graham looked like he wished he hadn't heard that. For a moment or two he didn't say anything, but when Lewis handed him the cup he finally got it out. "They have. They've taken everything. The war's over. Queretaro fell almost a month ago, on May fifteenth."

Slocum exchanged a glance with Greenleaf. He'd been expecting that. He'd known it as soon as he'd seen Graham's face and the way Brown had avoided meeting Lewis's eyes. Lewis had just been settling himself across the fire from Graham. Now he halted in a crouch, one hand still reaching for support. For a long moment he stayed poised in midair; then, his face pale above the gray of his beard, he slowly lowered himself to the ground.

"What about the Emperor?"

"Maximilian was taken prisoner," Graham said. "He's being held in the Convent of Santa Teresita in Queretaro, along with Prince Salm-Salm and his generals, Meija and Miramon. Juarez is still in the north, in San Luis Potosi. Diaz is in control here. So far they haven't bothered us, but that may come."

Bradley had gone over to explain the situation to his Mexicans, but Slocum was watching Lewis. Lewis looked like somebody had hit him in the solar plexus.

"So all this was for nothing," Lewis said. "I should have known when we saw Juaristas in Vera Cruz. And Austrian ships off the coast." He looked around at the men he'd spent three months organizing, but his eyes didn't seem to register. "At least those ships are there. I suppose Maximilian's to be taken into exile."

"It's worse than that," Graham said. "He's to be put on trial. Along with Prince Salm-Salm and the generals. Rumor is, it's a sham to justify a firing squad."

"They wouldn't dare." Lewis was bristling with indignation. "Maximilian's the brother of the Hapsburg Emperor. He's related to half the royalty of Europe. They wouldn't dare kill him."

"They intend to," Graham said. "Princess Salm-Salm's been in Queretaro trying to save them for weeks now. She's even gone to see Juarez in San Luis Potosi. The man insists Maximilian be tried. And if he's tried, a conviction is certain."

Bradley had returned to face Lewis across the fire. "Now at least we know it for a fact. Let's cut the play-acting and go back where we came from. You can't do any good now."

"No," Lewis said. "Now we're even more important. This small group of men is all that stands between the Emperor and a firing squad. We'll contact the princess in Queretaro and learn what we can. If necessary, we'll assault that convent and break the Emperor out."

"You're a damned fool," Bradley said. "This is a lost cause. Just like the last one. I'm taking my men back to Paso del Sol."

"Major Bradley, I forbid you to leave." Lewis rose to his feet, hands trembling, face close to red from anger. "I am still making the decisions here. We will go on to Queretaro and see what the situation is."

Bradley said something short and quick in Spanish. The Mexicans rose in a line behind him, loudly working the levers on those Henrys. Standing in that line, rifles at the ready, they looked like a firing squad themselves.

"Everybody just sit tight." Bradley's eyes swept the men in front of him. "I'm taking my bunch out of here. I'm through with this crap."

Slocum stopped his hand halfway to the Colt on his hip. He'd seen the Mexicans readying their rifles, but not in time to catch what was coming. A quick glance around showed him twenty-two men on this side, most of them still sitting, and about the same number facing them, armed for action. He caught Greenleaf's eye. Greenleaf shook his head ever so slightly.

"Now," Bradley said, "just so nobody's feelings

get out of line, suppose you gentlemen sort of disarm yourselves. Starting with the colonel there. Lay your weapons on the ground and back away till you feel that wall behind you. And don't anybody get brave. These boys of mine have done a lot of killing. They won't mind doing more."

Slocum watched Lewis ease his head around for a look at the men beside him. What he saw evidently didn't encourage him. Carefully, he unbuckled his gunbelt, laid belt and holster on the ground, and backed away.

"Very wise," Bradley said. "Now I'm going to be busy, but I'm leaving some men here to make sure you behave. Just follow the colonel's lead, and won't none of you get hurt."

He turned on his heel then and stalked away toward the trees the mules were picketed in, waving half the Mexicans off the line to follow him. One of those left said something in Spanish and waggled his rifle at Graham, and Graham carefully removed a pistol from his pocket. Warily, Slocum watched Bradley barking orders at the men he had taken with him. Two of them had pulled the picket stakes and were leading the mules forward. The others started separating pack-saddles out of the pile the guards had been posted on. Bradley was taking those Henrys with him.

Slocum was the fourth man to lay his gunbelt on the ground and back away with his hands raised. One Mexican had left the line and was retrieving each man's weapon as it was laid down. The first of the mules was being loaded. When Slocum felt the wall touch his back he found himself between Lewis and Graham.

"He won't shoot us, will he?" Graham said.

"Bradley?" Slocum said. "If I thought so, I'd never have given up my gun. Mexicans or no Mexicans."

"We pose no threat to him," Lewis said. "He just wants to get away clean."

"I wouldn't do anything to rile him, though," Slocum said. "The man's a little itchy. We want him to leave us our guns and horses."

"I trust Major Bradley will do that much," Lewis said. "He may be corrupted, but he is not evil."

When the Mexicans had the mules loaded and the horses saddled, Bradley came back out of the trees, carrying his rifle. "I'm pulling out," he said. "I expect you're staying, Colonel, but any of you smart enough to know when you're licked are welcome to come with me. You're safer travelling with me than you will be later. And leastwise you'll be getting closer to Vera Cruz and the coast. You can catch a ship there back to the States."

For a moment nothing happened. From the corner of his eye, Slocum saw Lewis looking straight ahead: he didn't want to see if one of his men was thinking of turning tail and siding with Bradley. Then from along the wall to the right a man stepped forward, one of those Lewis had brought aboard the *Gulf Queen* at Corpus Christi. He had no more than come to a halt when five others moved out from the wall to join him.

"Glad to see somebody's got some sense," Bradley said. "All right. Go find your weapons and mount up. Anybody else?"

While those five headed for the trees, careful not to look back, Bradley scanned those still standing along the wall. After a bit, another man stepped out— Grubb, the one Greenleaf had brought in as far back as the *River Queen*. Then another man stepped out, and then another.

Slocum kept his back snug up against the wall between Graham and Lewis. The sun was beginning to get hot overhead. A little gust of wind blew dust in his face. He reached up to wipe the sweat out of his eyes and caught Greenleaf looking at him from down the wall on his left. Greenleaf grinned wryly; they both knew Bradley was right, but Greenleaf would no more desert Lewis now than he would himself.

A few more men joined those heading for the trees. Bradley waited a bit longer. Then: "All right, gents. I made you the offer. I'll leave your weapons and one mule with the horses. I think you're fools, but it's your game. Luck to you, anyway." And he turned on his heel again and walked away.

Nobody moved. Slocum watched Bradley mount up and trot to the head of his little column. The column moved out, the mules jerking at the ends of their lead ropes, the packsaddles lurching and swaying heavily. Slocum waited till the last mule was out of sight, then stepped away from the wall.

He took off his hat and wiped a forearm across his face. "Well, maybe if there's any Juaristas around he'll draw them off."

"That's a thought," Graham said.

Slocum saw now that only Brown and Hodges remained of the men Lewis had brought with him. He exchanged a glance with Greenleaf: a pitifully small bunch—seven men half lost in this godforsaken country, looking to snatch one man out of the midst of thousands. And doomed to a firing squad themselves if they failed. Five men, likely, if Graham took that young Mex he'd brought with him and went back into Mexico City.

Lewis went to pour himself some now-cold coffee as if nothing had happened, but Slocum noted he had placed himself facing the hut. He didn't want to look at where those men had disappeared. If you listened close you could still hear Bradley's column dwindling in the distance. Over that faint sound came a crackling of brush from closer by: Hodges had gone into the trees and was on his way back, leading their horses and the one mule Bradley had left behind.

"I appreciate your staying, gentlemen," Lewis said. "Appreciate it more than I can say. I know things have changed. You signed on expecting to join a functioning army. Well, we're on our own now. We have to do what we can. Like I told Bradley, we'll go on to Queretaro." He turned to Graham. "Is there some way we can contact Princess Salm-Salm?"

"That's why I brought Juan here with me," Graham said. "Juan'll guide you. He's been running messages between the Princess and me ever since she went to Queretaro."

Slocum had retrieved his gunbelt out of the mule's packsaddle and was strapping it on. "Can he speak English?"

The young Mexican nodded solemnly. "I speak English, señor."

"Speaks it quite well, actually," Graham said. "He'll get you through the Juaristas all right. And you don't actually have to go into Queretaro. Not to meet with the princess, at any rate. She's staying with friends at a hacienda just outside the city."

Lewis was buckling his own gunbelt around his waist. "How much freedom of movement does she have?"

"They're treating her with every respect. She's had

complete access to the prisoners. And she's been very effective so far. She persuaded Juarez to postpone the trial till legal counsel could be obtained. Maximilian will be defended by one of Mexico's best lawyers, the father of the general who captured him."

"Not likely to do him much good. From what you say, he's as good as convicted already." Lewis poured the last of the coffee over the coals and turned to take his horse from Hodges. "But the princess can tell us the layout of the convent they're being held in. When worse comes to worst, we'll have to break into that convent."

Slocum didn't like that prospect: entering a city totally occupied by the enemy and grabbing their prize prisoner from under their noses. "What's our chance of getting into the city? We got to worry about that first."

"It would be possible only at night," the young Mexican said. "And then only in some form of disguise. You are too obviously *Norte-Americanos*. The Juaristas would stop and question you for that reason alone."

"We'll handle that problem when we come to it," Lewis said. "When does the trial begin?"

"Day after tomorrow," Graham said. "The twelfth of June."

"How long will it take us to get there?"

"Nearly a week."

"We'd better get started, then." Slocum stuck a boot in the stirrup and swung up into the saddle. "And we better hope that trial lasts a while. We won't do Maximilian any good getting there after he's dead."

11

It took them six days to reach the valley where Queretaro was situated.

Every day brought Lewis new strength. He felt a sense of purpose he hadn't had since the early days of the war, before Gettysburg, when it seemed sure the South would bring the Union to its knees. Queretaro was where he would free the last protector of that once glorious Confederacy, where he would deal a final blow for the old lost cause. His only fear was that they might arrive too late, with the trial over, the sentence handed down and carried out, the Emperor already dead, his own last reason for living gone.

He rode head down at the rear of the column, keeping his fear to himself. Juan, the young Mexican Graham had sent to guide them, took them over heavily wooded mountains and through dense, jungle-like gorges, never once travelling on what might be called a road. At night, bedded down under some luxuriant tree spreading its limbs out to twice its size, Lewis would wake out of sleep still trembling from a dream of Maximilian standing blindfolded before a wall, head up, hands bound behind him, a Juarista firing squad facing him in a single rank, the officer's sword raised in that final instant before the order to fire. This dream came to him every night, and always he snapped awake at just that instant: the sword raised, Maximilian's head up proud and erect to receive the muskets' fire. Lewis would lie awake for at least an hour then, listening to the breathing of the others and the strange sounds of the Mexican night, trying to convince himself that the dream was not an omen, was nothing more than an overactive imagination weakened by too much loss. Nonetheless, he was happy to see that valley opening out below when they came down out of the hills at sundown on the sixth day.

Queretaro was still several miles ahead. Juan led them down into the valley, into lush farmland and fruit orchards—olives and figs, grapefruit and oranges. After a while they turned up through an orange grove toward the red-tiled roofs of a house barely visible in a grove of trees—the hacienda of the Montoyas, Juan said. They were approaching it from the rear; Juan said Montoya was a known conservative, a supporter of Maximilian, and since he was sheltering Princess Salm-Salm in his home, there might be Juaristas around to keep an eye on it.

Juan had them dismount fifty yards behind a set of whitewashed adobe outbuildings and go on foot to the rear of a stable. They left their mounts in the trees and crept inside to a dim straw-strewn runway between two rows of stalls. Through a pair of double doors standing open at the front Lewis could see the white crushed stone of a gravel drive. Beyond the strip of white gravel was an adobe wall, and behind it trees in what was evidently a garden, and the house rising up to its sloping red-tiled roofs.

"You must wait here," Juan said. "It is safe here. The stableman is my friend. He will warn us if anyone comes. I go to see if things are safe at the house."

Juan trotted out through the runway and disappeared around the front corner of the stable, evidently looking for the stableman. Brown and Hodges slumped gratefully to the floor, and Hodges uncorked a canteen. Lewis joined Slocum and Greenleaf at the rear door, where they were gazing out at the low ring of hills that circled the valley.

"Hard to believe Maximilian brought his army down in here and went on the defensive," Slocum said. "All the enemy's got to do is occupy those hills up there."

"Exactly what happened, too," Greenleaf said. "Forty thousand Juaristas up there. And nine thousand Imperial troops trapped down here like rabbits in a sinkhole. Every position they had in range of Juarista artillery."

"Nonetheless, they held out for three months," Lewis said. "Granted, the Emperor had little battle experience. Probably he had bad advice, too, but you can't fault his courage. He could have abdicated. He could have fled back to Europe when the French deserted him. He chose to stay and defend his throne."

From behind them came Brown's sharp whisper: "Get down. There's somebody coming."

The three of them turned and ducked down against the wall. The stretch of white gravel out front was empty. Now Lewis heard horses coming from somewhere on the left. Probably the drive extended around the house. He heard a rattle of wheels and the squeaking of a coach on its springs and realized it had to be a team. A man's voice rose above the sound of the hooves, speaking to the horses, and now Lewis saw the team, two matched pairs of bays, pull to a halt in front of the stable door. The driver spoke to the horses as they nervously backed and filled, and then Juan emerged from the gate behind the house and crossed to enter the stable, followed by an elegant, elderly gentleman in a white suit.

"I have brought you Señor Montoya." Juan said. "All is safe here. Señor Montoya is happy to make you his guests. He is a great friend of the Emperor."

The elderly Montoya bowed stiffly and shook Lewis's hand. "You are welcome here, my friends. Juan tells me you have come very far."

Lewis introduced the others. He was impatient, trying vainly to read that polite and aristocratic Mexican face. "Sir, I'm eager for news," he said. "Is the princess here? Do you have any news of the Emperor? Is the trial over?"

"You must come with me," Montoya said. "The princess will meet with you in the courtyard."

Some rapid-fire Spanish sent Juan back to bring the horses in out of sight in the stable. Curbing his impatience, Lewis followed Montoya across the gravel drive, where the driver was down off the coach and opening up the rear boot. In the tile courtyard, Montoya directed them to wicker chairs under the shade of an arching palm and went into the house. A moment or two later, the princess emerged, wearing a travelling cape. Lewis watched her cross the courtyard, beautiful as ever, carrying herself with all the spirit and grace of a natural aristocrat. Hard to believe she'd been born in Vermont and had once been a circus rider. Harder still to believe that the Prince, a Prussian, youngest son of the ruler of Anholt, had been a general in the Union Army during the War. But allegiance to Maximilian wiped all slates clean.

He rose from his chair to kiss her hand and introduce her to the others. "Wonderful to see you again," he said. "Tell me everything. Is the Emperor alive? Has the trial ended?"

"The Emperor is alive. Please sit down, gentlemen. There's no need to stand for me. You've come a long way."

"I hope not too late," Lewis said. "Or with too little. We had four dozen men and a boatload of weapons till a week ago. But maybe there's enough of us to do something. Tell me what's happening. Tell me everything. How's the trial going? Does it look bad or good?"

"The trial is over." The princess took his hand in both of hers and pulled him down into a chair beside her own. "The sentence was read to the prisoners at ten this morning. Death by firing squad. To be carried out at three this afternoon."

Lewis felt a surge of grief crowding his throat. He started to speak, but she raised a hand to stop him.

"We're not beaten yet, Colonel. The execution's been stayed till the nineteenth."

"A stay of execution." He found it almost too much to take in. "Then there's still hope. Maybe Juarez is preparing a pardon. The trial has made his point. Maybe now he'll let the Emperor abdicate with honor."

"I'm afraid not. It's a short stay only, so that Maximilian can write a will and last letters to his family.

But don't give up, my friend. I'm leaving immediately for San Luis Potosi. Perhaps this time Juarez will relent. He's not an evil man, only obstinate."

The late sun lay soft on her cape. Long shadows stretched across the courtyard to where a small fountain splashed in a shallow pool. Lewis felt a momentary grief. This was what he'd lost with the War, what he'd hoped to regain here in Mexico—the gentle life of the South, on the great estates, surrounded by beauty. It was no longer possible. The least he could do was save the man who'd tried to make it possible.

"Juarez rejected your appeals before," he said. "Maybe it's time for direct action. These men have agreed to free the Emperor by force if necessary. You know the situation in Queretaro. You're allowed to come and go as you please. Would you help us?"

"I'm sorry. I'm afraid I can't help. I had hoped too to make an escape possible. I tried to bribe the officer of the guard, a Colonel Palacio. Unfortunately, he reported me to his superiors, and my pass was revoked. I've been banished from the city."

"Ah," Lewis said, "I'm sorry to hear that. Nevertheless, you've been in and out of that convent. You've seen how things are in the city. Do you think five men could get in there by night and take the Emperor out?"

She thought a bit. "It's possible. But I would prefer you didn't. If you failed, I'd have lost all chance to win Juarez over. I must try. At the very least, I might win my husband a pardon."

"But you do think it possible. If we agreed to wait till you've seen Juarez, could you describe the convent for us? Draw up a map?"

"Yes, certainly. If you agreed to wait, of course."

"Good," Lewis said. "Who has something to draw with?"

A pencil and paper were sent for from the house, and the princess set about drawing a map of the convent and the surrounding streets. The Emperor had been moved to a different convent, she said, the Convent of the Capuchins. And a previous bribery attempt had caused the Prince to be transferred to the city casino, in another part of town. Lewis knew they would never be able to free him. Two operations in one night would never succeed; it was necessary to concentrate on the Emperor.

There were two entrances to the convent—the main entrance on the west, another through a courtyard on the east. Maximilian was being held in a small room on the second story, off a balcony overlooking the courtyard. Juarista troops were billeted everywhere, the princess said: in the corridors of the convent, in the courtyard; the only way in would be to get up on the roof somehow and cross to the courtyard balcony. Because the balcony was in sight of whatever troops were billeted in the courtyard, only one guard was kept there. Late at night it might be possible to overpower him without attracting attention.

"I believe it's possible," Lewis said. "I believe it's worth a try. How about you, gentlemen?"

"I'm willing to find out," Slocum said.

"We came this far," Greenleaf said. "Might as well."

Lewis looked to the princess. "You understand, my first duty is to the Emperor. With the prince separated from him, it probably won't be possible to free them both."

"Yes, I understand. We can only do what is possible for each of us. But there are three days yet. Perhaps Juarez will relent."

"How will we know whether you succeed?"

"Today is the sixteenth. The execution is set for seven o'clock in the morning on the nineteenth. If you've not heard from me by dark on the eighteenth, you must go ahead with your plan." She gathered up her gloves and rose from her chair. "Pray to God it doesn't come to that. Now you will have to excuse me. I must go."

Montoya had come out to see her off. With him was a Mexican woman, evidently a servant, also wearing a travelling cape and carrying the princess's handbag. They left the cool of the courtyard and went out onto the drive, where the setting sun threw long shadows across the gravel. Juan lingered in front of the stable, talking to the stableman. The driver had finished loading the baggage into the boot and stood now by the open door of the coach. Montoya murmured something to the princess, bowed, and kissed her hand.

Now Lewis stepped forward and kissed her hand also. "Godspeed."

"Thank you. You must pray that I succeed. If I fail, you know I shall be praying for your success."

She mounted up into the coach. When the servant woman had joined her, the driver shut the door and clambered up into the driver's box. He flicked the reins and the team jerked into the traces. The coach lurched and swayed on its springs. Then it was moving out along the white gravel drive, a faint film of dust rising up behind it. It circled the corner of the house and disappeared.

"There goes a strong woman," Lewis said. "It's a

shame she arrived in Mexico too late to meet the Empress. Carlota was every bit as strong, an impressive woman. Many believed she would have made a brilliant ruler in her own right."

"What happened to her?" Greenleaf said.

"She sailed to Europe last fall to plead with the French and Belgian kings for assistance. She never returned. They seem to be shielding the Emperor from the truth, but the rumors are very bad. Some say she's dead, others say she's gone mad." He watched the dust slowly settle to the white gravel again, heard the coach receding away down the road. "Let us hope the princess is able to charm Juarez this time."

"Gentlemen, if you will forgive me." It was Montoya, bowing with aristocratic courtesy. "I'm afraid it is not safe being out in the open like this. I shall have to ask you to stay in the stable loft. Juan will see to your needs and warn you if any Juaristas appear."

"Of course," Lewis said. "We're very grateful for your help. I hope we bring you no trouble."

"You bring me no trouble. I am very appreciative of what you do for the Emperor. But in the meantime we must make sure you are safe. Please follow me. I will show you the way to the loft."

12

The afternoon of June eighteenth passed with no word from Princess Salm-Salm.

Slocum was standing at a small loft window when the sun started sinking behind the hills to the west. Long shadows stretched away from the trees in the orange groves outside. In the hay behind him Lewis was propped against a ceiling support, reading a book he carried in his pack. Juan was out somewhere scouting the country, but the other three were lying in the hay at the other end of the loft playing jawbone poker with a set of cards Montoya had sent out from the house. Slocum had grown very bored with jawbone poker; he figured another day or two of this and the whole bunch of them would have cabin fever.

They had holed up in this loft for the entire two days, coming down only in the dark to stretch their legs. They couldn't have a lantern, for fear of alerting

Juaristas, so they'd had to turn in soon as dark fell every night, sleepy or not. And there was nothing to do during the day except sit around playing cards for money none of them had and waiting for mealtimes, when Juan carried a heavy pot of beans and tortillas out from the house and told them what bits of gossip he'd been able to pick up around the countryside. Once each day, shortly after noon, Montoya had come out from the house and gingerly climbed the ladder into the loft to ask after their welfare and see if there was anything they needed, but other than that the days had been unbroken stretches of tedium.

Slocum had watched Lewis grow more impatient with every passing hour, still hoping some messenger would arrive from San Luis Potosi to say the princess had won a pardon from Juarez. Slocum figured there wasn't going to be any pardon; the only thing on his mind was getting out of this loft, even if it meant going into Queretaro and snatching Maximilian out of the midst of the Juarista army.

Now he heard the gate squeak behind the house and turned to see Brown struggle through the hay to the window at the other end of the loft.

"It's Juan," Brown said. "He's got supper."

"Good." Lewis clapped his book shut and got to his feet. "It's time. He should know by now if there's any word from the princess."

Slocum got a coil of rope from his gear and went to crouch in the hay at the head of the ladder. Down below, Juan caught the end of the rope and tied it to the handle of the pot he carried, and Slocum hauled it up. Lewis had joined the others getting their mess kits out, as if this were just another mealtime, but he couldn't hide the eager interest in his face when Juan came up the ladder.

Juan came over to join the group hunkered down around the pot of tortillas and beans. Slocum could read the news in that immobile peasant face.

"No word?" Lewis said.

Juan shook his head. *"Nada."*

Hodges was dishing the tortillas and beans out of the pot. He handed Lewis a full mess kit, but Lewis was staring off into space. Slocum took a mess kit from Hodges and found Greenleaf looking at him from across the circle.

"Looks like we're going to have to go in after him," Greenleaf said.

"Yes," Lewis said. "Yes, I'm afraid so." For the first time he seemed to notice the mess kit in his hand. "I'd hoped the princess would have better luck, but now there's no alternative."

"You been thinking on what to do next?" Slocum said. "Luck'll decide whether we get Maximilian out, but Juan says we can't even get in there 'less we disguise ourselves some way."

Lewis was scooping beans into his mouth with a tortilla. "You remember that abbey we passed coming down into the valley?"

"No, I can't say I do."

"Stone building set back among some trees. Had a cemetery behind it. Up on that rim of hills to the south."

"I remember it," Greenleaf said.

"I've been thinking," Lewis said. "The Church is a powerful force to these people, even to liberals like the Juaristas. If we can get some priests' habits from that abbey, I suspect we can enter Queretaro with no trouble. Even the liberals are too superstitious to interfere with a priest."

Slocum considered it. "Is the Church on Maximilian's side? Would they cooperate with us?"

"Afraid not. The Emperor is Catholic, but as a ruler even he was too liberal for the Pope. Besides, they wouldn't help armed Americans obviously bent on trouble. We'll have to take what we want at gunpoint."

"Sounds all right to me," Greenleaf said.

"That's best anyway," Lewis said. "That way nobody can blame them for anything. We'll get started soon as we finish supper. We'll have to find that abbey again and subdue whoever's in it, then make our way into the city. We want to get in there after midnight, but not too long after."

Two hours after nightfall they were out of the valley and climbing up into the hills again. They had gathered up their gear after supper and climbed down out of the loft and saddled up their mounts while Juan took the heavy pot back into the house. He was accompanied back out by Montoya, cordial and courteous as ever, who wished them well and assured them they could find safe haven here again if they needed it. Slocum figured the old gentleman had to be happy to see them leave, but he didn't show it.

Lewis sent Juan away on his mule ahead of the rest, heading back to Mexico City to tell Graham Princess Salm-Salm's mission had failed and that they were going to try freeing the Emperor by force. Once Juan was safely away, Lewis led them back south through the orange groves, under cover of the dark now, staying off the roads. Slocum was glad to be out of that loft, out in the night air, with a sense of this thing coming to a close at last.

He was following close behind Lewis when Lewis reined up and passed back word to halt. They had topped the rim of hills and turned west some time back, strung out single file, passing through trees. Lewis was in the lead, aiming toward where he remembered that abbey to be. The moon had come up at dusk, thin and wan, and now that they were stopped, Slocum could see the pale line of a low stone wall angling left up ahead. Off to the north, beyond where the ground dropped away, far out in the valley, he saw the lights of Queretaro.

"We're close, I think," Lewis said.

He reined left and eased his horse along the wall, under low-hanging tree limbs. Slocum followed. The only sound was the slow, muffled thump of hooves. Now he saw the dim white of headstones receding away in rows beyond the wall. They'd found the graveyard behind the abbey.

Lewis had halted again. Saddle leather creaked as he turned. This time he kept his voice to a whisper. "You see anything?"

Slocum moved his horse up. For a long moment he stared through the dark. Then he saw it, maybe fifty yards ahead: the dark bulk of the abbey, rising two stories up into the night. "Dead ahead," he said. "Across a stretch of grass. There's some kind of building off to the left of it, too, not as big."

"You better take the lead," Lewis said. "My eyes are getting old. Can't see very far in the dark any more."

The others had closed up behind them. Greenleaf

nudged his horse up alongside Slocum's. He had his Colt out and was checking the cylinder. "Anybody in there likely to be armed?"

"Possible," Lewis said. "The Church likes Juarez even less than it likes Maximilian. Could be they've taken in refugees from Queretaro. They'd probably be armed."

Slocum dismounted and drew his own Colt. "Hodges, you hold the horses here. The rest of us'll handle whoever's inside. We'll be coming in the front. Better be ready in case we flush anybody out the back here."

Hodges dismounted to take the reins. On foot now, Slocum led the rest of them along the wall toward the back of the abbey, keeping low. When he reached the corner of the wall he went down on one knee. The building on the left was closer—not as tall as the abbey, the dark maw of a big entry standing open on this side. Now he saw some sort of conveyance in front of it, a buggy or a cart. He had no doubt it was a stable. The rear of the abbey was dark, but he saw a glow of light around to the right of it. Somebody had a lamp lit, and the light was spilling out a ground-floor window.

"Colonel, you and Brown go up along this near side and around front. Greenleaf and I'll circle around and see where that light's coming from. I doubt anybody's out this time of night, but be careful. We'll meet you somewhere around front."

He waited till Lewis and Brown had moved across that stretch of grass and ducked behind some shrubbery at the side of the building. Then he waved Greenleaf forward and moved out along the wall to the right.

The lamplight was coming from a window up near the front of the abbey. He could see it had iron bars over it, bolted to the stone of the building. In a crouch, he circled around wide till he was beyond reach of the light stretching across the grass and slowly rose up till he could get a look in.

A fat priest sat at a desk just inside, his back to the window. Facing him across the desk stood a thin, wiry man in what Slocum took to be a monk's robe. The light was coming from lamps somewhere out of sight, and he didn't like that. If there were lamps he couldn't see, there might also be men he couldn't see.

Greenleaf was crouched in the dark beside him. "What do you think?"

"If it's just priests and monks, should be no trouble. Let's go around front."

Dark bushes stood at the corner of the building. Ivy crept up the stone of the front wall. Now Slocum could see a gravel lane stretching out through tall trees toward the road. He found Lewis and Brown crouched in some shrubbery just to the right of two stone steps leading up to a heavy wooden door with a brass knocker on it.

"Didn't see anything along the side," Lewis said. "Where's the light coming from?"

"Ground-floor window. Looks like the first room on our left as we go in. There's a priest and a monk in there, two men at least. Now I'm going to bang that knocker, and when the door opens, bust on in and fan out. Brown, you take whoever answers the door out of the way. The rest of us will take those two in the room. Then we'll search the whole place, fast, before they can recover from the shock."

"Try not to hurt anybody," Lewis said.

"Unless you have to," Slocum said. "Everybody ready? All right. Let's go in there."

He waited till they were crouched at the ready in the shrubs to either side of the door, Brown and Greenleaf on his left, Lewis on his right. Then he mounted the stone steps and rapped the knocker on its metal base.

There was no response from inside. He'd had his Colt holstered; now he drew it again—only for a show of force, if he was lucky. He waited a minute more and rapped again.

Still nothing from inside. But that door was likely too heavy to hear through. Now he heard the rattle of the latch. He glanced once to the others to make sure they'd heard, then put a hand and one boot against the wood of the door and braced himself.

The door opened maybe five inches. Above the flicker of a candle, the face of a short jowly monk wore a baffled expression. Slocum hit the door like a bull.

He slammed past the startled monk and ran for the room where he'd seen those two men. The door to it stood already open; he burst inside and found the fat priest rising open-mouthed from his chair behind the desk, the wiry monk wheeling toward the door. The priest said something in Spanish, heated and abrupt, and Slocum waved his Colt at him.

"Hold it. Just hold it. Stay where you are."

Lewis and Greenleaf bolted past and down the corridor and started snatching open every door they came to. The fat priest halted half out of his chair, still sputtering, and the wiry man was shrinking away, watching the muzzle of the Colt. Maybe they didn't know English, but everybody understood the language of a gun. Keeping an eye on them, Slocum turned to see Brown dragging the short monk along the corridor by his sleeve.

"Put him in here with these two and stand watch on them. We'll handle the rest."

He wheeled out of the room and started along the dark corridor after Greenleaf and Lewis. On his right, a narrow staircase led up to the second story. He could hear doors still being opened around a bend in the corridor, but nothing that sounded like trouble. Then he saw a flicker of light up ahead, and encountered the other two coming back his way, Greenleaf carrying a candle.

"Nobody down here," Greenleaf said. "Nothing but offices and pantries and such like. Found some candles in the kitchen. Everybody's likely in bed upstairs."

"Then let's get up there," Slocum said, and vaulted for the stairs.

They found twelve men upstairs, all in bed, most asleep, some of them awakened by the noise below. There were a lot of baffled and sleepy queries in Spanish, but none of them resisted, and there were no refugees from Queretaro, nobody armed, and nobody inclined to cause any trouble. Lewis used what Spanish he had to calm them down, and when it came clear there was going to be no resistance, Slocum relaxed and allowed them to dress. Eight of them were monks, wearing robes, and three wore the cassocks of priests. When they were dressed, Slocum herded them downstairs to join the three Brown was standing guard on.

The fat priest started jabbering in Spanish again, and that set the others off. The room was a sudden jumble of noise, everybody talking at once. Slocum shouted and knifed through the crowd and brought his Colt up under the fat one's nose.

"I said shut up."

The priest shut up, sat sullenly down in his chair, and glared at Slocum. The jabbering from the others stopped like somebody had slammed a door on them.

Slocum said, "Brown, take 'em into the next room and get these priests to strip. Fatso here, too. When you're finished, lock 'em in. If that room doesn't have bars on the windows, find one that does. Colonel, I think you better write Maximilian a letter. Something to let him know who we are once we get into his cell."

Brown was herding the monks and priests out of the room, barking at them in Spanish, shooing them along with his pistol. Greenleaf had gone out to tell Hodges he could bring the horses in. Lewis, about to sit at the fat priest's desk, looked at Slocum with surprise.

"Surely there's no need for that. We'll all go in together."

"We can't. I figured on using the priests' outfits, not monks' robes. Priests wear that wide-brimmed hat you can shield your face with. We got four priests, four cassocks. We need one cassock for Maximilian to wear on his way out. Means only three of us can go in."

"Possibly so, but I intend to be one of them." Lewis sat down at the desk, a quill pen leaking ink on a stack of manuscript paper in front of him. "I didn't come all this way to withdraw at the last minute. We can leave Hodges and Brown here. They can guard the monks."

"Colonel, with all due respect, you're not a young

man any more. According to the princess, that convent is three stories high, and the only way in is up the side of it and over the roof. We're going to have to do it fast. If something happened to you, we'd lose all chance of getting the Emperor out."

Lewis lowered his eyes to the desk, like maybe he was letting that sink in. Slocum figured it was hard for him to swallow, but it was true and necessary to be said; he didn't want to be climbing the side of a building with a man nearing sixty.

"Very well," Lewis said. "I'm forced to see the truth of what you say." He picked up the quill pen and selected a sheet of paper. "I'll provide you with an introduction and let the Emperor know what we plan. He speaks English, so you'll have no problem there."

"Good," Slocum said. "Greenleaf and I'll go in. We'll take Hodges with us. Brown can guard those priests while you try to figure a way to get Maximilian out of this country. We're going to need a plan for that."

Greenleaf came back with Hodges, who had stalled the horses in the stable they'd passed on the way in. When Brown came back in, Slocum unbuckled his gunbelt and started getting into one of the priests' cassocks.

"Better carry your gunbelts till we climb that wall. Might run into trouble on the way in. Can't get at a gun fast under a cassock."

Greenleaf already had his gunbelt off and was trying to figure out how to get the cassock on. "There ain't nothing in that stable but a burro and an ox cart. We'll have to go in in the cart to look genuine."

"It'll do," Slocum said. "We'll have to stick to the

roads, but we want to look genuine. You better put Maximilian's cassock on under the other one. Be hard enough climbing a stone wall without having something to carry."

When they were dressed, Lewis sealed his letter with some sealing wax he'd found on the desk and came to give it to Slocum. "Tell the Emperor we hoped to be here in time to join his fight. Failing that, we've come to free him. Tell him we have not forgotten, those of us from the Confederacy to whom he gave shelter."

"I'll do that. We'd better go now. It's getting late."

Lewis shook his hand and reached for the hands of the other two. "I wish I could go with you, but I understand. You're right. I might make things more difficult. The important thing is to get the Emperor free."

"We'll do our best," Slocum said. "If he can be got out of there, we'll get him out of there."

13

They were four miles west of the abbey when they saw the Juarista checkpoint.

They had been moving along at a steady walk, the ox cart's wooden wheels squeaking rhythmically, Slocum flicking at the rump of the stubborn burro with a long willow switch he'd found in the cart bed. Then he saw the glow of a lantern through the trees about a hundred yards ahead, just beyond where the road forked. One branch angled left there, likely toward Mexico City; the other bent gradually to the right, starting downgrade into the valley. In the pool of lantern light to the right of the road stood two soldiers in Juarista uniforms, each of them carrying one of General Sheridan's Henry repeaters.

Slocum kept the burro moving at a walk. "Any ideas what to do? They've already seen us, so we can't turn back. And we're in a mess of trouble if they stop us. Don't none of us speak enough Mexican to pass."

He felt the cart shift as Hodges turned to look over his shoulder. The soldiers ahead separated, one of them crossing from right to left to flank the road. Now another came down out of the trees where the lantern was and joined the first one, watching them come on.

"Maybe if we take the left fork, they won't bother us," Hodges said. "They're probably only checking people going in and out of Queretaro. We could circle around and find another road in."

"Likely every road's got a checkpoint on it," Greenleaf said. "Might as well try this one. If the colonel's right, they'll let us pass when they see these priest outfits."

"Maybe they're just looking for Imperial army stragglers," Hodges said.

"Maybe."

Carefully, keeping an eye on the soldiers up ahead, Greenleaf felt around at his feet and handed Slocum the Colt he'd stashed there. Slocum laid it on the seat beside him and draped the skirt of his cassock over it.

Now Greenleaf brought up his own pistol and held it out of sight down along his thigh. Without turning around, he said, "Pretend you're asleep, Hodges. Pull that hat down over your eyes, but make sure you can see what's going on. We may have to shoot our way out of this."

Slocum flicked the burro once and set the willow switch down. Holding the reins in his left hand, he rested the edge of his right hand on the seat just under the skirt of his cassock, where he could get at the Colt.

They were close enough now to get a better look at the soldiers. The one on the left, his rifle on a sling over his shoulder, looked no more than nineteen, but the two on the right looked experienced enough. Slocum saw one of them turn to say something to the other, then laugh and turn back to watch the cart come on. Greenleaf was slumped down on the seat, the priest's hat practically covering his face. Slocum had his own hat pulled low over his eyes, hoping the brim would keep his face in shadow, and he was careful to look straight ahead, past the burro's bobbing head. Then the cart was coming up even with the soldiers; he saw the young one on the left make the sign of the cross, and then they were past and the burro plodded on, head bobbing, and Slocum heard the Juarista laugh again. He felt a familiar tingling at the nape of his neck, but he didn't turn his head.

Behind him, Hodges whispered, "Looks like we made it."

Slocum allowed himself a careful look around. The one doing the laughing had disappeared back up into the trees. The young one was ambling back across the road. Only one of them was still watching the ox cart.

He turned back to the front and tipped his hat up and started fumbling with the cassock so he could get at his makings. "Close call. Anything started, we'd have had to shoot all three. Luck's with us so far."

"Thank God for the power of the Pope," Greenleaf said. "Switch up that burro. Let's get in there and get this over with."

Midnight had come and gone by the time they reached the outskirts of the city. Having been in Queretaro with the colonel once, Hodges traded places with Greenleaf, figuring he could guide Slocum to the convent. Though most of the buildings were dark, the city itself seemed alive and noisy. Half the Juarista army looked to be here, and like any troops still flush with victory, nobody wanted to sleep. Soldiers roamed the streets in bunches, some drinking, some drunk. None of them paid much attention to an ox cart carrying three priests.

The princess had said the corridors of the convent were crowded with the families of the guards. That arrangement seemed common among the Juaristas: every now and then the ox cart passed whole companies billeted in the streets, many of them with wives and children bedded down around campfires built right on the cobbles. The buildings still showed signs of battle—roofs shattered, cornices crumbling, walls chipped up by bullets. Here and there Slocum saw a house which had been totally destroyed by artillery. They passed a large plaza turned now into a campsite for a cavalry company, the horses gathered in a rope corral at one end, three rows of tents stretching down the middle. Then Hodges directed him up an alley to the right and then left again onto a cobbled street, and up ahead Slocum saw another company billeted around small fires on the cobblestones.

"I think that's it," Hodges said. "That wall on the right. I think that's the convent."

Slocum pulled the ox cart to a halt in the shadows at the curb about a block back from the troops. This company too had wives and children with them, but most looked to be asleep. Several of the soldiers were awake, smoking and talking, standing around the iron gates leading in through a high stone wall on the right. The wall stretched the length of the block the troops were billeted on and cut right ninety degrees at both ends of it. Slocum could see a strip of grass and trees flanking the wall where it disappeared up the next side street.

"That drawing showed those gates at the east end of the courtyard," Greenleaf said. "Convent should be facing the street a block over. I don't cotton to passing through them Juaristas, but we ought to look at all four sides of it."

"We'll swing a block left and go around," Slocum said. "We can skip this end. It's for sure we ain't getting in through those gates. Let's hope the other sides ain't so populated."

He tugged on the reins and backed the burro along the curb till they could cross back through the alley and circle around south and west again. When they passed the other end of the block the Juaristas were camped on, he saw that the soldiers were still clusted in front of those high iron gates. Then they were across that street and moving along the dark side of the convent wall. There were no troops here. Another twenty-yard-wide strip of grass and trees separated the street from the wall. Now Slocum saw trees inside the courtyard, too, and firelight flickering against the underside of their branches.

"Fires inside the courtyard," he said. "Must be another infantry company billeted in there."

"Might make getting onto that rear balcony a little difficult," Greenleaf said.

"Well, we'll know when we get up there."

There was a third infantry company in front of the convent, complete with campfires and families bedded down around them. Slocum saw more officers here, standing around the main entrance to what had become Maximilian's prison. Then they were across this street too, and they circled around the next and came back again. The block along the north wall of the courtyard was as empty as the other. Slocum scanned the convent as the burro ambled past: a two-story main building fronting the street they'd just crossed, a lower stone extension reaching partway back toward the street in the rear, and then the wall surrounding the courtyard. Climbing up onto that extension would be easiest, but the only thing he could see to get a rope on was a large stone cross rising up from the peak of the gable on the main building.

Greenleaf had seen it too. "We can put a rope around that cross up there. If it holds, we can climb the wall up onto the roof and get a look at what to do next."

"What happens if somebody from the courtyard sees us?" Hodges said.

"Why, then we'll be in trouble," Slocum said. "We'll have to make sure that don't happen."

Twenty minutes later they were standing at the bottom of the convent wall, in amongst the trees on the strip of grass bordering the street. They had stashed the cart in an alley between two squalid tenements six blocks away and made their way back on foot through the dark. The streets were empty; Slocum figured the area around the convent was off limits to any but the soldiers guarding it. Greenleaf had the cassock for Maximilian on under his own; he and Hodges crouched against the wall while Slocum carried the rope back a ways and shook out a loop.

His first cast fell short, the rope skittering back down the wall to land with a thump in the grass. The next time the loop settled over the cross. He snugged it down tight and leaned on it, hard, till he was sure it would hold. Then he heard horses approaching east along the street.

Greenleaf hissed. "Patrol coming. Riders, anyway. Better hug the ground."

Slocum dived for the grass along the base of the wall, head to head with Greenleaf. He was glad they were posing as priests; the black of the habits should give them some protection in the dark. He still had the end of the rope with him, but there was no way to get the rest of it off that cross fast enough.

The horses were coming closer, their hooves ringing on the cobbles. He had his hat over his face; now he nudged the brim up and peered through the sparse trees toward the street.

It was a patrol, or soldiers anyway, four of what looked to be Juarista cavalry. They passed by at a slow trot, moving in and out of view through the trees. When they had passed on by, he used the rope to pull himself to his knees.

"Lucky that time," Greenleaf said. "Might have been different if one of us was halfway up that wall. Let's hope our luck holds."

"The rope holds," Slocum said. "that's the first thing. I'll go first. Send Hodges up next. Then you." He leaned back on the rope, placed one boot against the wall, and started up.

The wall seemed higher than it had from the ground. By the time he approached the level of the second-story window, his arms ached from the strain. The window was directly in his path, the rope stretched across the length of it. When he neared the sill he started edging sideways, moving up around the side. He had almost made it past when his boot slipped out from under him.

He caught himself just in time. He landed hard with one knee against the stone at the upper corner of the window, his boot just inches away from the pane. He clung there for a moment, listening, waiting, trying to ignore the pain in his knee. The scrape of his boot against the stone had seemed very loud, but no reaction came from inside. Painfully, he pulled himself up till he could get both feet on the wall again, hauled himself up to grab that cross, and pulled himself over onto the tiled peak of the roof. He lay there a moment, breathing hard. Then he waved down to tell Greenleaf the way was clear and turned to scan the courtyard below.

Gravel walks, flower beds, patches of grass, with tall trees scattered through it all. There were maybe two platoons billeted down there, but they were all asleep, curled up with the usual wives and children around a dozen dying fires. The convent with its two extensions to the rear was shaped like a U. The roof obscured all but one small stretch of balcony, along the end of the wing extending back on the right, and he could see outside stairs angling from there down into the courtyard. There was no sign of a guard.

When Greenleaf and Hodges made it up over the gable, Slocum coiled up the rope, leaving the loop around the stone cross, and carried the coil down the roof far enough to avoid being silhouetted against the sky. The other two were hunkered down on the tiles, watching the courtyard.

"Everybody's asleep," Hodges whispered. "That's one thing in our favor, anyway."

"You seen the guard anywhere?" Greenleaf said.

"Not yet," Slocum said. "I figure he's back under the balcony roof somewhere."

The rear extension on this side thrust back from the main building ten yards down on their left, creating a shallow V where the two roofs joined. A drainage tile sloped down the center of it to a gutter along the eaves. Slocum could see a short stretch of balcony rail just below that gutter: the corner where the balcony bent back on itself.

"Look," Hodges said. "There's the guard."

Now Slocum saw him, too: a single man in a Juarista tunic and a wide sombrero, strolling out of the dark along that stretch of balcony visible over on the right, his rifle on a sling over his shoulder. The man halted at the end of the balcony, gazing down the outside stairs into the courtyard.

"Don't nobody move," Slocum whispered. "He's got to turn back this way. If everybody's still he won't see us."

The guard stood with his back to them for a good five minutes. Slocum held so still he could hear the sound of Greenleaf's breathing, right beside him. From the street behind the courtyard came the sound of horses, loud on the cobbles, and he saw four more cavalrymen pass the iron gates back there. Then the guard turned and ambled back along the balcony till he disappeared under the dark of the roof.

Slocum listened. The man's footsteps faded a bit, turned, and came along the rear of the main building. They grew louder as he neared the corner below the V of the two roofs, then turned again and faded slowly up toward the other end of the balcony. Then they stopped.

Slocum laid the coil of the rope on the tiles and began pulling his boots off. "Sounds like he's bored. I bet he takes that little walk every five minutes or so. Next time he passes us down there, I'll see if I can take him."

"You figure on doing it alone?" Greenleaf asked.

"I'll have to hang on to the end of this rope to keep on the edge of the roof. Only room on the rope for one. I'll drop behind him. One ought to be enough. Hold these boots."

By the time he heard those footsteps start back he was lying on the edge of the roof, gripping the gutter with one foot to stay horizontal. The rope stretched taut up the roof to that stone cross, holding him where he was. He had his Colt out, and it was all he could do to hang to the end of the rope, coiled up as it was, without losing his grip. He heard the footsteps approach along the side balcony, slow and casual. They halted once, briefly, then came leisurely on. They neared the corner, turned, and passed just below him. He took a deep breath and swung down over the gutter.

He hit the balcony lightly, on his toes, but even that was too loud. The guard was barely five feet away, already turning, startled face coming around, hands fumbling for the rifle slung over his shoulder. Slocum crossed those five feet with a single stride and brought his Colt down hard on the crown of that big sombrero.

He caught the man as he sagged and lowered him quickly to the floor, going down on one knee himself. He was breathing hard, too hard to hear if the other man was breathing, and he had to fumble for a pulse to make sure he hadn't killed him. Nobody had stirred around the fires down in the courtyard. Several soldiers were still clustered outside the rear gates, but nothing looked unusual out there. He heard a sound behind him and turned to see Greenleaf drop off the end of the rope and crouch down behind the balcony rail.

"Good work." Greenleaf came along the rail to him, bringing his boots. "Hardly heard a thing. He alive?"

"He's alive. Got a hard head."

Hodges was down off the roof now. Still on one knee, Slocum scanned the shadows under the roof. There were three doors off each of the side balconies. Six led off the balcony he was on, into the rear of the main building. If the princess was right, they would find Maximilian off the center door of the six. He felt along the belt the guard was wearing till he found a single large key on a metal key ring. Likely that one key fit all twelve of those doors. He slipped the key ring off the guard's belt and beckoned Hodges away from the rail.

"Stash that rope up in the gutter so nobody sees it hanging down. Then take that cassock off and put this fellow's tunic and hat on. I want you to take his place out here."

Slocum dragged the guard over to the middle of the balcony, so Hodges could keep an eye on him. When he had the rope stashed, Hodges struggled out of his cassock and put the Juarista tunic and sombrero on. Slocum figured he would pass from a distance. If somebody got close enough to see him, it wouldn't matter anyway.

"We don't know when this man was due to be relieved," he said. "His relief would likely come through the gates and up the outside stairs back there. You see anybody, rap on the door. Maybe we'll have time to get over that roof before they can react."

Hodges didn't look too happy about this, but he

took the guard's rifle and faced out over the balcony to watch the gates at the rear. Slocum moved to where Greenleaf was waiting by the entrance to what should be Maximilian's cell.

The door was made of thick, heavy wood, bound with iron straps, too snug against the jamb to show whether there was any light inside. Slocum ran his hand along the jamb till he was sure the door opened inward, then eased the big key into the lock, careful to make no sound.

"Can't say I'm too happy about this," he whispered. "Might be another guard or two inside the cell."

Greenleaf had his back to the wall on the other side of the door and was watching the fires down in the courtyard. "Figure it this way. Any guards in there'll think it's this one opening the door. First thing they'll see is two priests come to tend to Maximilian. Time they learn otherwise, we ought to have the situation in hand."

"You know, if it don't go that way, there ain't much chance of our getting out of here."

"I was hoping you wouldn't remind me. Open the door, and let's get this over with."

Slocum put his own back to the wall on his side of the entrance. Shifting the Colt to his left hand, he slowly turned the key with the other till he heard the click of the latch. Then he placed his outstretched fingertips against the door and pushed it gently open.

14

The heavy door swung inward. Slocum watched the faint starlight advance across the floor as the door swung all the way back against an inside wall. There was no light inside the cell. If there were any guards in there, they were keeping awful quiet. He switched the Colt back to his right hand and eased around the doorjamb till he could just see in.

The outline of a bed was barely visible in the corner to his right. Also to the right, catty-corner across the dark room from him, was another door, likely leading out onto an interior corridor. He could see a small judas window in that door, where the guards would look in to check on whoever was in the bed. A bend in the wall straight ahead created a small alcove in the near corner, in which he could see the dark bulk of what looked to be some kind of chiffonier.

Hodges was watching nervously from the balcony

rail. Greenleaf had slipped in to put his back to the open door, his Colt out, the black of his cassock making him almost invisible. Slocum stepped all the way inside. To his right he discovered a small table. He felt around on it till he found what he'd been hoping for: the heavy metal of a candlestick, with a candle already stuck in it.

"I found a candle. Close the door and I'll get it lit."

Greenleaf removed the key from the lock and eased the heavy door shut. Slocum got one last glimpse of Hodges's scared face before darkness blotted it out. Then he fumbled a box of lucifer matches from a pocket under his cassock and groped in the dark to find a place to lay his Colt down. When he had both hands free, he got the match lit and touched it to the candle's wick. The flame's weak and quivering glow gradually spread around the walls of the cell. Holding the candlestick in one hand, he picked up his Colt again.

Between him and the bed in the corner was a table and two chairs. A few bottles of wine, two of them empty, were all that remained of a meal. Beside the bed was a nightstand with another candlestick on it, and beside the candlestick a thick leather-bound Bible. The man in the bed was lying on his back, sound asleep, wearing a nightshirt. He looked a good deal better than six feet, with a very thick, blond beard parted in the middle and spreading like wings away from his chin. From Lewis's description, Slocum had no doubt it was Maximilian, archduke of Austria, younger brother of the Hapsburg Emperor, son-in-law of the King of Belgium, until recently himself Emperor of Mexico.

"Look at him," Greenleaf whispered. "Due to be shot in the morning, and he's sound asleep."

"Better go put your ear to that other door," Slocum said. "May be more guards in that corridor out there. We don't want them looking in on us."

He put his Colt and the flickering candle on the table beside the wine bottles and moved to the bed. He was surprised to see that Maximilian wasn't very old, maybe thirty-four or thirty-five. Greenleaf laid his ear to the door; he listened for a beat or two, then signalled an all clear. Slocum leaned down and shook Maximilian by the shoulder.

Maximilian's eyes flicked open immediately. Slocum watched those eyes take in the black of his cassock, the cross on the chain around his neck, the figure of Greenleaf standing in another priest's cassock at the door. A stricken look passed across the Emperor's face. Then he got control of himself and rolled up to one elbow. Quickly he made the sign of the cross.

"Ja es tiempo?"

"You'll have to talk English," Slocum said. "And quiet, too. We're not what we look like. We don't want any guards learning we're in here."

Startled, Maximilian sat all the way up in the bed. Even here, imprisoned in this small room, he wore a fine linen nightshirt, with ruffles at the throat and wrists. "You are not priests?"

"No, we're not," Slocum said. "Are there guards in the corridor outside? Do they look in on you at night?"

Maximilian wiped a hand across his eyes. "There are guards. They look in regularly. I can't say how regularly after I'm asleep." Now he saw the Colt in Greenleaf's hand, the riding boots just visible beneath the hem of Greenleaf's cassock. "If you are not priests, who are you?"

"This'll tell you who we are." Slocum brought Lewis's note from the same pocket he'd had the matches in and handed it to Maximilian. "If my friend there hears any guards coming, he'll give a signal. If he does, I'll slip back into that alcove, but I want you to take that Bible and pretend you're reading it. That'll explain the candle to any guard looking in. I know you got to get clear on what's happening, but we'll have to do it fast. The place is swarming with Juaristas."

Maximilian had been reading the note; now he lowered it to his lap and looked at Slocum, something like bewilderment in his eyes. "You're from Colonel Lewis? You've arranged an escape?"

Slocum thought he heard a sound in the corridor. He looked to Greenleaf, but Greenleaf shook his head.

"I'm not sure I'd put it that way. We didn't know you'd lost to Juarez till about a week ago. Weren't even sure you needed rescuing till we talked to Princess Salm-Salm. This is a pretty makeshift operation."

"You have spoken to Princess Salm-Salm?"

"Three days ago. She was on her way to San Luis Potosi, trying to get Juarez to rescind your sentence. We agreed if we didn't hear from her by tonight we'd get you out of here."

That news seemed to hit the Emperor a little hard. "She has failed, then. With Juarez, I mean."

"Looks like it," Slocum said. "'Less you know something we don't."

"No," Maximilian said. "No, I know nothing. And I am not surprised. You see, you are not the first to visit me tonight. The Juarista general, Escobedo, came to bid me farewell shortly after twelve. I knew then the princess had failed. But I cannot complain. She has been very diligent. She has done for me everything within her power. It was not her first plea to Benito Juarez on my behalf. The man is determined I should die."

"We've got other things in mind," Slocum said, "but we'll have to move fast. Colonel Lewis is waiting for us outside the city. We'll have to take you out the way we came in—climbing over the roof and down the north wall. And you'll have to hide under a pile of sacks in the ox cart we rode in on. Least till we can shave off that beard and dye your hair or something. You think you can make it down a three-story wall on a rope?"

The Emperor seemed not even to have heard; he was looking at Slocum as if struck by something curious. "You are an American. A *Norte-Americano,* we would say here. Like the princess. How does it happen that you, an American, are attempting to help me?"

"Colonel Lewis recruited us. We fought under him during the War. Our War. We lost that one, too. The colonel's very loyal to you, sir. I know he'd want us to get you out of here quick as we can."

Maximilian bowed his head graciously, as if this were some sort of royal audience. "I am deeply grateful. I am only sorry the members of the Carlota Colony were forced to leave Mexico. And now Colonel Lewis wishes me to leave Mexico as well, does he? You say I'm to hide under sacks in an ox cart till we are outside the city. What arrangements have been made for leaving the country?"

"Colonel Lewis is working on that, sir." Slocum

had the odd feeling he was talking to a man in a dream. This was no time to play Emperor. "The colonel mentioned something about trying to go north, make our way overland to the States or back to the coast at Vera Cruz. We sighted at least two Austrian warships cruising those waters."

"Sent by my brother, no doubt. Dear Franzl. Perhaps he regrets the differences between us." Maximilian seemed to be musing. "Fleeing through the streets in an ox cart. I am not happy with that image of myself, gentlemen. The picture is perhaps too familiar. In the revolt of 1848 we were twice forced to flee Vienna. The second time so unexpectedly we were able to secure only one carriage in which to convey the entire royal family. Franzl and I rode post horses on either side to shield the carriage from the mobs. Old women—children, even—shouting for our deaths. I was sixteen at the time. A humiliating experience."

"There'll be nothing like that," Slocum said. "We either get away unnoticed, or we don't get away at all."

He was beginning to wonder if the Emperor wanted to get away. Maximilian seemed in no hurry to move. Slocum looked to Greenleaf at the door, but Greenleaf just shrugged.

Maximilian was still reminiscing, as if happy to have company. "Charlotte's grandfather, Louis Philippe of France, was forced to flee his capitol in Forty-eight as well. My wife, you know. Colonel Lewis's Carlota Colony was named for her. She was haunted by the image of that. Royalty fleeing its own subjects through the streets. It would never do to be caught hiding under sacks in an ox cart like a common thief."

"Better than a firing squad, I'd think," Slocum said, trying to jolt some sense into the man. "I hear a firing squad's how they plan to do it tomorrow."

"For an Emperor," Maximilian said, "there are things worse than death."

"Hssst. Slocum. Somebody coming."

It was Greenleaf, stepping abruptly aside to flatten himself against the wall in back of the door. Slocum wheeled, snatched his Colt off the table, and faded back into the dark of the alcove. He watched as Maximilian quickly took the Bible from the nightstand and lay back on his pillow. Footsteps approached along the inner corridor and stopped.

After a short pause, the little judas window was flung suddenly open.

Slocum held his breath. He couldn't see the door. The corner of the alcove put even Greenleaf out of sight. Maximilian had the Bible propped open on his chest and seemed to be reading. Now he raised his eyes and gazed back at whoever was peering in at him.

A long silence. Maximilian dropped his eyes back to the Bible. Slocum waited, listening for the rattle of a key in the lock. Then the judas slammed shut again and the footsteps went off along the corridor.

Slocum waited. Maximilian still appeared engrossed in the Bible.

Then Greenleaf murmured from the door, "He's gone."

Slocum stepped swiftly back to the bed. "You've got to be quick now. They see you're reading that Bible, they may just send for a real priest. Or something may go wrong outside. The courtyard down there is full of troops. We got one man posted out on the balcony, and that's all there is of us. We got to get out before anybody knows we're here, or we'll never make it."

Greenleaf was back at the door, his ear placed against the wood. Maximilian had laid the Bible face down in his lap.

"What about my generals? Generals Meija and Miramon. And the prince—Prince Salm-Salm. Could we—can they be rescued as well?"

"Where are they?"

"Meija and Miramon are in separate rooms on either side of me. The prince has unfortunately been removed to the casino, in another part of the city. He was discovered trying to bribe the guards in another escape attempt."

Maximilian had his eyes on that Bible. Slocum had the feeling the man didn't want to look at him, didn't want to see what the answer to that question was going to be. Greenleaf was shaking his head at the door, but Slocum didn't need to see that to know what to say.

"We could maybe take the generals with us. Be a tight fit in that ox cart, and awful risky, but we could try. But not the prince. There's not enough time. We'd have to find out where he is, how to get in, how to get him out. It's just not possible."

Maximilian was silent for the length of a breath. "Yes. Yes, I can see that. Not possible. Yes." Then he laid his head back against the pillow and closed his eyes. A shadow of something, almost a twinge of pain, passed across his face. "I cannot go, gentlemen. I cannot flee and leave those closest to me facing that firing squad alone."

Slocum wasn't sure what to say to that. After a

long moment, Maximilian opened his eyes and looked up at him. From the door, Greenleaf said, "You better be sure. We can pretty well guarantee getting you out of here."

"That's right," Slocum said. "If we get out, you get out, and I for one sure aim to get out of here."

"I appreciate the risks you've taken, gentlemen, but I must refuse your offer. In these few weeks of battle, the prince became a great friend to me. He did not have to be here. His allegiance to me was his only cause. I will not desert him now."

"Maybe Juarez will at least grant him a pardon," Greenleaf said. "Seeing as it wasn't political reasons he was fighting for, and he'd only been here a couple of months."

"No. He was tried under the same article I was: a charge of aiding what Juarez calls 'the foreign intervention.' The princess has taken his case to Juarez before. I do not expect her to succeed now."

"Hold it," Greenleaf said. "Somebody coming again."

Quickly, Slocum moved back out of sight behind the alcove. Maximilian took up the Bible again. The sudden nighttime silence seemed to ring in the room, and in that silence Slocum heard the sound of footsteps approaching again along the corridor. Two sets of footsteps this time.

The guard and who else? Slocum hoped the second man wasn't a priest. Surely a priest would come to this cell before Maximilian was led out at dawn. Please, God, not now.

The footsteps halted outside the door. Again Slocum held his breath and listened for the rattle of a key in the lock. Maximilian was watching the door. Abruptly, the shutter over the little judas window was thrown open again.

Again there was that long silence. Slocum listened to his own breathing, so loud he was sure it could be heard all the way to the door. Carefully, he crept to where the alcove opened out into the main room and pressed himself to the wall there, ready to spring in case that key sounded in the lock. Greenleaf would be poised behind the door. Together, the two of them might be able to jump whoever it was. It would have to be quick, and quiet—a gunshot would bring troops swarming up from that courtyard outside.

From the corridor came a muffled murmur of voices—question and response, two men speaking Spanish. Silence. Then another exchange, and then silence again.

Then the shutter slammed shut and the footsteps receded along the corridor.

Relieved, Slocum holstered his Colt and stepped out of the alcove to see Greenleaf listening again at the door. Maximilian had crawled out of his blankets and stood beside the bed now, tall and very much the Emperor, his nightshirt reaching all the way to the floor.

"That was the chief guard," he said. "They might be going now to Colonel Palacio, the officer in charge. Everyone is very tense. Under the circumstances, someone may come in to check on me. You had better go now. And quickly."

Greenleaf came over from the door. "There's still time for you to get some clothes on. This is your last chance. You know that. It's for sure the prince would want you to escape, even if he can't."

"Very likely," Maximilian said, "but I cannot. The honor of a Hapsburg forbids it. It is better this way, gentlemen. I failed here. I failed at the one thing that had meaning to me. I no longer have a throne. My dearest Charlotte is dead or, worse, mentally unbalanced—no one seems certain which. Please go before it is too late. And tell Colonel Lewis how deeply grateful I am for his loyalty."

Slocum held out his hand. "You're a brave man, sir."

He remembered then that the man was an emperor, and likely you didn't offer your hand to an emperor. But Maximilian smiled and shook his hand, then offered his own to Greenleaf.

"It is you who are brave men, gentlemen. You and Colonel Lewis. Please do convey my last respects to the colonel and to Princess Salm-Salm."

"We'll do that," Slocum said. "Any other messages we can take out for you?"

"Thank you, I have sent messages to everyone due them. I think you should go now. Please be careful. I would not want you harmed on my account."

"You mind if I take a bottle of wine?" Greenleaf said. "We left an unconscious guard out there. I want him to smell like he drank himself that way."

"By all means. Take whatever you find useful."

Greenleaf tucked a bottle under one arm and led the way to the door. "Better douse that candle. We don't want anybody in the courtyard seeing the light when we open this thing."

"Very well."

Maximilian picked up the heavy metal candlestick and saluted them as if the candle were a glass of champagne. Greenleaf inserted the key in the lock, and Maximilian blew the candle out. The last Slocum saw of him was that pale face just above the candle, the thick blond beard, and the white nightshirt—all of it fading into total darkness. Then Greenleaf unlocked the door and they stepped outside.

15

The balcony was bathed in blue moonlight. Slocum waited for his eyes to adjust, watching for movement in the shadows along the side balconies. The fires were dying in the courtyard below. A vague figure in a wide sombrero moved out of the dark to the right of the door, giving him a start till he was sure it was Hodges.

Even in the moonlight Hodges looked a bit pale. "Thought you were never coming out of there," he whispered. "Where's the Emperor?"

"He's not coming," Slocum said.

"Not coming?"

"Wouldn't leave unless we could get his generals and the prince out." Greenleaf had locked the door again and was on his knees beside the unconscious guard, returning the key ring to the man's belt. "You have any trouble out here?"

"That fella there started moaning and stirring around. I hit him another good one 'crost the head. You mean he's going to stay here and just let himself be killed? Maximilian, I mean?"

Slocum was scanning the courtyard and what little of the street he could see through the gates. Everybody in the courtyard seemed to have rolled up in their blankets, but there was a small cluster of soldiers just beyond the gates. "Tell the truth, I don't think he wanted to escape. His big brother runs the whole Hapsburg Empire. Half the world over there, if I remember my schooling. This was his chance to make good on his own. I think he'd rather die than go home a failure."

"All this way for nothing," Hodges said. "The colonel's not going to be happy."

"We'll worry about that later," Greenleaf said. "Even the colonel can't keep a man from dying if he wants to die. Better get that uniform off and the cassock back on." He had uncorked the bottle he'd brought from Maximilian's cell and was spilling wine on the guard. "This way maybe nobody'll believe him saying he was knocked out. Then they won't come looking for us even when they do find him. Fish that rope out of that gutter and let's get out of here."

They made it up off the balcony and over the roof with as little trouble as they'd had coming in. Slocum was the first to walk the wall down the rope to the ground, and while waiting for the other two he knelt in the shadows under the trees and watched the streets for Juaristas. The air was cool at this hour, almost cold. June, but high country, where the air got thin. He heard voices from around the far front corner, from those troops on the street, and he looked up the rope, anxious to be gone. Then Hodges was down, and he saw Greenleaf halted about ten feet up.

Greenleaf was propped feet first against the wall, clinging to the rope with one hand. Now he brought a knife up in the other and cut the rope, quick and clean.

He hit the ground hard. It took him a moment to get to his feet, but he was all right. He put his knife away and started rolling up the length of rope he'd brought down with him, watching the rest of it swaying above his head. "Nobody'll see that till morning," he said. "Let's get to that ox cart."

It was close to four A.M. when they neared the checkpoint in the hills west of the abbey. Everything had gone fine so far. They'd got away from the convent without being seen and had found the ox cart unmolested in the alley where they'd left it. Nobody had stopped them or questioned them on the way out of the city. They'd encountered one mounted patrol on the road up into the hills, but that patrol had simply passed them by once it was clear they were wearing cassocks. Now the lanterns of the checkpoint glowed through the trees ahead. Slocum was at the reins. From the corner of his eye he saw Greenleaf bring his Colt out and hold it down along his thigh. His own Colt was on the seat between them, under the skirt of his cassock.

"Checkpoint coming up," he said. "Keep your eyes and ears open, Hodges."

Softly, Greenleaf said, "Let's hope it's the same ones we passed on the way in. If they recognize us, we should have no trouble."

Then they were too close for talking. One of the soldiers stepped down to the edge of the road. Slocum caught a glimpse of another getting to his feet up in the trees. The first one had his rifle on a sling over his shoulder and was watching them come on. Slocum kept his head down, as if half asleep, his eyes watchful under the brim of his hat. Then the first soldier nodded once and waved them through.

Slocum heard the second man call out something from the trees. He held his breath till they were out of earshot; then, to Hodges, without looking around, he said, "What's happening back there?"

"One of them was jawing at that one that let us through," Hodges said. "Maybe he got suspicious. He's let up now. Went back up into the trees."

"We've made it," Greenleaf said. "If they really suspected something, they'd be after us by now."

"Remind me to thank those priests before we clear out," Slocum said.

There were no lights showing when they got within sight of the abbey. Likely Lewis had decided lights would draw unnecessary attention at this hour of the night, but Slocum was taking no chances. He sent the burro up the gravel lane at a walk, watching the shadowy dark under the trees, listening for unusual sounds. There seemed to be nothing out of the way; he saw no new hoofprints, heard nothing suspicious. The ox cart creaked around the side of the abbey, and the burro quickened its pace, sensing it was home. Slocum decided he was expecting trouble where there was none, and his mind moved now to where the real trouble would be: Lewis. He didn't want to think about how Lewis was going to take the news. But that was none of his affair. They had done the job, and the Emperor had refused to come, and that was all any man could ask. That Lewis might ask more, that Lewis might by now have more invested than he ought to in this was something Slocum didn't want to look at.

He figured Greenleaf and Hodges were thinking the same thing. Neither of them said anything when he pulled the burro to a halt in the hay-smelling dark of the stable. Silently, they followed him toward the rear of the abbey, cassocks brushing the already dew-wet grass.

As he rounded the rear corner, he heard a muffled voice from up ahead: "Slocum? Greenleaf?"

"Brown? That you?"

"Heard you coming up the lane. Wanted to make sure it was you." It was Brown, standing in the dark of the half open door. "The colonel's waiting inside. Where's the Emperor?"

"No luck getting him out. You got a light? Can't see where I'm going here."

"I got a candle. Step in here so I can close the door on it."

Inside, the door closed, Brown struck a match and lit a candle and led them off down the corridor. Greenleaf removed his hat and caught Slocum's eye, looking grim, but neither of them said anything. The room they'd locked the priests in was silent and dark. Then Brown stopped and opened a door and ushered them into the office.

Lewis was seated behind the desk. Slocum watched his eyes track them into the room: himself, Greenleaf, Hodges, then Brown. Nothing changed in that gray-bearded face when the door clicked shut behind them, and yet Lewis seemed abruptly an old and very tired man.

Brown put the flickering candle on the desk and went to light another one on a bookcase against the wall. Slocum shucked the cassock and took a seat in the first of four chairs in a row in front of the desk. He saw a dusty bottle of wine at Lewis's elbow, still corked, with six wine glasses grouped around it. Lewis must have searched out the abbey's wine cellar, planning a toast to Maximilian's escape.

Brown leaned against the wall. The others shucked their cassocks and sat beside Slocum. One chair remained conspicuously empty.

"Welcome back, gentlemen," Lewis said. "I see you're alone. I'm sorry. Were you able to get anywhere close?"

"Got right into his cell." Slocum said. "Could have brought him out with us, but he refused to come. Said he wouldn't come unless we freed his generals and the prince, and there was no way we could break the prince out in time."

Lewis stared at him. "He wouldn't come." It wasn't a question; he seemed to be repeating it to make sure he understood. "You got into his cell, you could have brought him out, but he wouldn't come."

"That's right, sir," Slocum said. "Said he wouldn't leave the prince to face that firing squad alone. I think he was glad to have an excuse to stay. I think he figures dying tomorrow's what history or fate or something meant for him all along."

Lewis closed his eyes, like maybe he was gathering strength. He looked very tired. When he opened his eyes again he said, "Did you show him my note?"

"He read the note. Said to tell you he was grateful for all you'd done. 'Deeply grateful for your loyalty,' I think he said. And to pay you his respects."

"Tell me the whole thing," Lewis said. "From the

beginning. A full military report. I want to know everything you encountered."

Slocum gave him a detailed report: about the checkpoint at the road junction farther west, about the patrols they'd passed, the layout of the convent, the guard they'd left for drunk, the severed rope left hanging. If a regular report gave the man a sense he'd done his duty by whatever military code he still lived by, Slocum figured he deserved one.

But when he finished, Lewis said, "We've got to go back and get him out. The opportunity is still there. We must force him to leave if necessary."

"Sir, it won't help trying a second time," Slocum said. "He had a clear chance to leave and he refused it. And by now that guard's come to and reported what happened. Likely they've found the rope. We couldn't get back in there if we wanted."

"We will try nevertheless." Lewis was getting heated and close to anger; his face was flushed above that gray beard. "You made sure the guard appeared drunk on duty. By now he's in irons himself. They'll have seen the prisoners are still there; they'll have no cause to search for anything like a rope. At least, we can't quit till we find out they have."

Slocum could see Lewis had his mind made up; if he wasn't stopped now, he could get them all in trouble. "With all respect, sir, I won't go with you. It's a fool's errand, and it'll just get good men killed."

"I agree," Greenleaf said.

Lewis stared at them, like maybe he didn't believe what he'd heard. His eyes were flat with anger. "Very well, gentlemen. I'll go without you. Hodges, give me your cassock. You're about my height."

Hodges flushed, looked to Slocum. "No, sir, I reckon I won't. You'd just be getting yourself killed for nothing."

"Hodges is right, sir," Brown said. "You can't go back. Even by yourself. We'll have to stop you if you try."

Lewis bowed his head. For an instant Slocum thought he was praying, but he knew it wasn't that. The colonel was trying to keep his emotions in check, trying to accept news he hadn't wanted to hear.

Now Lewis nodded. "I suspected as much." Slowly he rose from his chair, the pistol suddenly coming visible as his hand cleared the desk top. "I'm afraid you've made this necessary. I respect your judgement, gentlemen, but I'll not let you stop me. You know me to be a serious man. Believe me when I say I'll put a ball in any man who tries. Now I'll be a lot less nervous if you'll place your firearms on the floor. Carefully."

Slocum looked at Greenleaf and Greenleaf shrugged. Slocum knew it didn't matter: none of them would shoot Lewis to stop him, anyway. Carefully, he unbuckled his gunbelt and bent to lay it on the floor at his feet and stepped back a bit while the others did the same.

"Now bring me your cassock, Hodges," Lewis said.

Hodges flushed and hesitated and looked to Slocum again. He seemed to settle something in his mind, picked up the cassock, and moved toward the desk.

Everything happened too fast for Slocum to react— almost too fast for him to see. Figuring to make his move when Lewis started for the door, he watched Hodges circle the desk. Lewis, his eyes on the rest of them, stuck out an arm, wanting the cassock draped over it. When Hodges got close, he lurched suddenly forward, looped the cassock around that arm, and yanked, pulling Lewis off balance, lunging for Lewis's gun hand, trying to grab the gun. He wasn't fast enough. Lewis brought a knee up quick and sudden and clubbed him over the head with the barrel of that pistol, and Hodges went down like a stone.

Slocum was caught flat-footed. He'd barely moved when Lewis had the pistol trained across the desk again.

The colonel was shaking now, likely shocked himself at what he'd done. "Sorry," he said. "Sorry I had to do that. Don't make me do worse. I'll shoot somebody if I have to, I swear I will, so don't push me. I'll shoot to wound, you know that, but I'm not sure how accurate I can be. Humor me, gentlemen. I'm an old man. Let me go. If I fail, I fail, but I have to try."

Slocum caught Greenleaf's eye and saw Greenleaf shrug: there wasn't anything they could do, not until they could catch Lewis off guard. He was going for broke now, and nothing much mattered anymore but trying to finish what he'd spent the past two or three months preparing for: trying to save Maximilian.

On the floor, Hodges rolled and groaned and put his hands to his head. There was no blood, but he had a rapidly rising bump on his skull. Keeping that pistol trained across the desk, Lewis edged to his left and bent to pick up Hodges's cassock and drape it over his shoulder.

"Stay on the floor, Corporal. You made a brave try. I'm sorry we've been brought to this." Now he began to move gradually to his right, along the back of the desk. "The rest of you go on over there and join him on the floor. Face down. I don't want to hurt somebody worse."

"You can't do it, Colonel." Greenleaf started circling around toward Hodges, hands up at chest height. "Even supposing you get back in there, you can't make him leave if he don't want to go."

"His generals will help," Lewis said. "The guard must have keys to their cells. They'll help me, even if it means we have to club him and carry him out."

Slocum was following Greenleaf. From the corner of his eye he saw Lewis come out from behind the desk, but he was too far away now and too much on his guard for it to do any good. Greenleaf eased down onto the floor beside Hodges. Slocum found Lewis waving the pistol at him to do the same. He picked a spot on the floor beside Greenleaf, went down on his knees, and laid himself out belly down.

"I'm sorry to have to do this, gentlemen," Lewis said. "God willing, I will be back here by dawn. If not, I trust you will eventually find your way out of here."

Slocum heard him move to pick up the gunbelts they'd left in front of the desk. Then footsteps moving toward the door, the click of the latch, the turn of the key in the lock.

Then Lewis's footsteps faded away down the corridor toward the rear of the abbey.

16

Greenleaf swore and rolled up to his feet. "We got to stop him, or he'll get himself killed."

"Got to find a way out of here first," Slocum said.

Hodges was getting up now, dabbing at his head with a handkerchief. On his feet again, Slocum stepped quickly round the desk and went to the one window. There would be no getting through the heavy iron grill bolted to the stone outside. Three of the walls were lined with bookcases. The floor was made of thick oak planks. The only door was the one Lewis had locked behind him.

"He took our guns," Brown said. "How can we stop him?"

"I doubt he took the rifles off the horses," Slocum said. "All we got to do is get close enough to shoot his mount out from under him. Or that burro if he takes the ox cart. Bring me that candle."

He pulled his knife from its scabbard in his boot and slipped the point of the blade into the keyhole on the door. The keyhole was pretty big; likely it held the same kind of large iron key they'd opened Maximilian's door with. He probed a bit till the knifepoint met resistance: the blunt end of the key. He removed the knife then. While Brown held the candle to one side, he bent and peered into the keyhole till he got some idea of the way the key was aligned. Then he thrust the blade in again and probed and pushed till he felt the key begin to give. Carefully he nudged it backward till he heard it fall from the lock and bounce on the floor outside.

"So far so good. Let's hope it didn't bounce out of reach. Let me have the candle."

He got down on his belly, holding the candle as low as it would go, and peered out under the door. The flickering flame cast a weak light maybe two feet out into the corridor, but he could see the key, just a faint gleam of metal at the farthest reach of the light.

"See anything?" Greenleaf said.

"It's out there. Only question is, can I get it back."

He rolled up to a sitting position, unbuckled his belt, and pulled it out of the loops of his pants. It was a thick, wide belt, the buckle maybe three inches across. Not the best thing to probe with but the only thing he could think of. He went back down on his belly, the candle at one elbow, and pushed the belt buckle out into the corridor.

Going straight ahead was easy enough; he pushed the buckle on till it was past the key. Trying to maneuver a flexible belt to the side was another matter, but the belt was a thick one and held its shape pretty well. On the third try he heard the clink of buckle meeting key. Then, very carefully, he began to draw the belt toward him.

He lost the key four times before he finally brought it within reach of his fingers. Each time, he worked the belt back into the dark of the corridor and eased it forward till the edge of the buckle caught the key again. When he finally had it in his hand, he got quickly to his feet, put his belt back on, and unlocked the door.

"Bring those candles," he said. "And make it fast. Be best if we can catch him before he gets too far."

They found the gunbelts where Lewis had left them on the floor halfway along the corridor to the rear door. One of the monks shouted something and pounded on the door as they passed, but they ignored him. On the way to the stable, Slocum looked beyond the cemetery in back and saw lights far out in the valley: lit windows in Queretaro, likely Juarista duty stations. The only other light came from the pale moon and the two candles bobbing through the dark ahead of him where Brown and Hodges were nearing the stable.

Greenleaf was tightening his saddle cinch when Slocum came into the dim candlelit stalls. "He took the ox cart," Greenleaf said. "Means he'll be going slow. Maybe we can catch him before he reaches that checkpoint. Seeing another priest out in the wee hours might make those boys suspicious."

Slocum loosed the reins of his own mount and led it out into the dark.

"Let's move," he said. "And make sure you see any Juaristas before they see you. We're not disguised as priests this time." Then he swung up into the saddle and spurred on out toward the road.

The ox cart had just reached the checkpoint when they caught up with Lewis. They were moving at a lope through the trees to the left of the road, using the grass to muffle the sound of hooves. Slocum was in the lead, watching the moon-pale road stretching away empty up ahead, the moon itself flickering through the treetops. The road stayed empty, and for the space of a heartbeat or two he was sure Lewis had made it on through; then he saw the lantern through the trees and one sentry moving down into the light and the dark bulk of the ox cart slowing and Lewis, indistinct in the black cassock and hat, gradually pulling the burro to a halt.

Slocum eased his mount down to a trot and reined up under a tree at the edge of the road. The horse shifted and danced; he had to haul back on the reins to get it quiet while the others nosed their own mounts up alongside him.

Brown was pulling out a pair of field glasses, steadying his horse with his knees while he brought the glasses to his eyes. Greenleaf had his rifle out and ready, and Hodges was feeding cartridges into the magazine of his.

"What do we do now?" Greenleaf said.

"We'll wait. Maybe he'll get past." Slocum turned to Brown. "You think the colonel's Spanish is good enough to get him through there?"

"If he thinks fast enough," Brown said. "He could tell them he's a European priest the Church sent over here. They wouldn't bother him if he could get them to believe that."

"What about papers? He's wearing your cassock, Hodges. It have any papers in it?"

"There were papers in side pocket," Hodges said,

"but I took it off a young priest, a Mexican. If they try to match the colonel with what it says on those papers, they'll nab him for sure."

Slocum reached for Brown's field glasses. "Give me those things. I want to see if he's got his papers out yet."

"Look," Greenleaf whispered.

Shouts at the checkpoint had already brought Slocum's head around. At first he saw a blur, then the ox cart in motion, lurching forward, Lewis slashing at the burro with his stick, the burro beginning to run. One guard was running for the trees above the road. Another was running after the cart, trying frantically to yank the rifle sling down off his shoulder.

Slocum drew his Colt and raked his mount with the spurs. "He's done it now. Come on, we got to take them before they take him."

Greenleaf had already kicked his horse into the lead. Slocum hit the road right behind him, no longer worried about keeping quiet, wanting the Juaristas to hear, wanting to draw them off that ox cart fleeing down the road.

Already he heard a staccato sputter of rifle fire and saw the flash of a gun-muzzle blast from up in the trees on the right. He fired a shot into the air, and Greenleaf poured three more into the trees. The guard in the road had got his rifle off his shoulder; he was standing spraddle-legged, taking aim after that ox cart, when he heard the firing behind him. He wheeled then and was bringing the rifle back up when Greenleaf dropped him with a single shot.

Slocum saw a horse burst out of the trees on the right, slashing down the slope to the road and cutting right after Lewis, the rider flogging it with a whip.

Another rider came down out of the trees, fighting his horse, the horse rearing and squealing and sunfishing; Slocum put a bullet in its hindquarters and saw it slam to the ground, throwing the rider, and then he was flying on past, leaving the rider to Brown and Hodges, cutting down the road after that third Juarista.

Lewis had got himself a bit of a lead, but it wasn't lasting; there was no way that burro could hold off a running horse. Slocum took a quick look around. Hodges and Brown were nowhere in sight. Greenleaf was holding even with him, just back of him, both horses stretching into a full-out gallop.

The sound of a shot blew back past him, then another. The Juarista was leaning along the neck of his horse, firing at Lewis. Slocum hauled his rifle out of the scabbard and levered a round into the chamber, watching the moon flick past over the Juarista's back, bringing the rifle down along the horse's ear, settling the sights between the Juarista's shoulders.

At first he thought he'd missed. Then the Mexican started sliding sideways. His rifle fell and bounced end-over-end and clattered off into the dark. The horse started to slow. The Juarista sagged from the saddle, one boot catching in the stirrup; he swung down like a rag doll, and his head hit the road and bounced. Then the horse was down to a jolting trot, dragging the man along the road, and Slocum burst on past, heading after Lewis.

Greenleaf had drawn up alongside him now. They were closing fast on the ox cart, and Slocum began to slow his horse. He could see Lewis was hurt, or worse: he was sprawled on the seat, not moving, the burro running loose. Slocum caught up to the burro and leaned down to grab the bridle and began pulling in on his own reins, bringing both horse and burro down to a stiff-legged trot before he got them halted.

Greenleaf was already vaulting from the saddle back by the ox cart; he ground-reined his horse, leaped up onto the cart, and went to feeling at Lewis's chest. Slocum was down out of the saddle now. He heard a horse coming at a run back up the road, but he saw it was Brown, and he jumped up to help Greenleaf.

Greenleaf had Lewis laid out along the seat. Lewis' face was as gray as his beard now, even in the moonlight. Greenleaf was feeling for a pulse at the base of the neck. Slocum couldn't see any blood, but with that cassock black as it was, blood would be hard to see in the dark. Then he saw blood dripping from Lewis's hand where his arm hung down off the seat; he reached to lay that arm up across Lewis's chest, and his whole hand came away wet.

Brown had stopped beside the cart now. Still in the saddle, breathing hard, he said, "Where's he hit?"

"Can't tell for sure," Slocum said. "Blood all down his front. He wasn't moving even before I got the burro stopped. How's his pulse?"

Greenleaf sat back against the seat-back and wiped his hands on the hem of Lewis's cassock. "He's got no pulse."

"He's dead?" Brown said.

"That's what I said. He's all shot up. Two or three wounds, all in the back and chest. I think one of them hit his heart."

In the long silence that followed, Slocum heard another horse trotting along the road and looked up to see Hodges coming, riding a Juarista cavalry mount. Brown had dismounted and was shakily rolling up a smoke. Slocum fumbled under his cassock and brought out his own makings. When Hodges reined up alongside the cart, he looked first to Slocum and then to Greenleaf, and Greenleaf shook his head.

Hodges looked a little stunned. "The colonel's dead?"

"Dead before we got here," Greenleaf said. "Shot in the heart. May have been dead before he got a dozen yards past the checkpoint. What happened with that last Juarista?"

"He shot my horse out from under me. But I got him, so we're square. I'm glad. I'm glad I got one of them. Even if it didn't help the colonel none."

Gunsmoke still hung in the air over the road, the smell strong and acrid. Slocum dug a match from his pocket and lit Brown's cigarette and his own.

"What are we going to do with him?" Brown said. "We can't just leave him here."

"I figure he's owed a decent burial," Slocum said. "That abbey's got a cemetery. Let's bury him there. Ought to be shovels around that stable somewhere. A little talking to them priests before we leave, maybe a little donation to the poor or something, ought to set things right. We didn't hurt none of them."

"We'll have to do something with them Juaristas," Greenleaf said. "Their relief'll be along before we're done. We got to steer them away from the abbey."

"I thought about that," Slocum said. "Brown, you and Hodges put the bodies on the two cavalry mounts still left and dump them about two miles down the road toward Mexico City. Leave a trail. Anybody hunting them will think we went on south."

Greenleaf turned his horse over to Hodges and took up the burro's reins, ready to turn the cart back toward the abbey. Slocum retrieved his own horse and swung back up into the saddle. Lying there in his cassock, the colonel looked like a real priest now, one who had finally gone to meet his maker.

Greenleaf was looking at the body, waiting for the horses to get out of the way. "Colonel Robert E. Lewis," he said. "He came a long way to die."

"Well, he died doing what he wanted to do," Slocum said. "We'll be lucky if people can say the same when we're gone. Let's get moving. We got a lot to get done before first light."

17

The crack of dawn was showing in the east by the time they finished the grave.

Slocum was doing the last of the digging. He worked out a final shovelful, heaved it up onto the mound of displaced earth, and tossed his shovel after it. Greenleaf leaned down to grab his hand and haul him out. Hodges blew out the lantern they had been using to see by. Lewis's body was laid out at the foot of the grave, a blanket from the abbey underneath him, another laid over him. Once up on solid ground, Slocum dusted his hands off and stepped over to one side of the body.

"Let's get him in there."

He and Greenleaf grasped the bottom blanket at the head and Hodges and Brown did the same at the foot, and together they moved the body up over the grave and went down on their knees to lower it gently in. When Slocum got to his feet, wiping the dirt off his knees, he saw the top blanket had fallen to one side, leaving Lewis's face uncovered. Lying there looking peaceful, the gray of his beard shining silver in the day's first light, Lewis had never looked more like his first hero, old Bobby Lee. And now here he was dead in the same country his second hero was soon to die in, an old forgotten soldier of an army that didn't exist anymore, exiled from a homeland that didn't exist anymore either, lying in ground that neither he nor Maximilian had belonged to but that both had tried to turn into some romantic homeland of the spirit, inveterate dreamers who'd found their dreams running right smack up against reality. So maybe it was best they both die here, in the final country of their dreams, before life could teach them any more harsh lessons.

He reversed his shovel and used the tip of the handle to move the blanket back across Lewis's face. Greenleaf was leaning on a second shovel stuck in the mound of fresh dirt. Hodges and Brown stood on the other side of the grave, looking down at the body.

"Anybody here a religious man?" Slocum said.

For a moment or two there was only an embarrassed silence. Then Hodges said, "I am, sir."

"You know any words to say?"

Hodges looked down at the body in the grave. Then he swallowed once. "No, sir, I'm afraid I don't."

Ranked rows of headstones were growing pale in the early light. From the trees around the abbey came the call of a mockingbird. Slocum could see morning mist hovering in the orange groves in the valley below.

"Anybody have anything he'd like to say?"

Brown took off his hat, reminding the others to

take off their own. "I can only say here lies a good man. A good officer. A man loyal to God and country, who asked only that his country love him back. I guess it's fitting he be buried here, on the morning his last commander-in-chief is set to be killed. I wish them both Godspeed."

"Amen," Hodges said.

"Amen," Slocum said, and put his hat back on. "Who's got a watch?"

Brown fumbled in a vest pocket and brought out a stemwinder on the end of a chain. He cracked open the lid and held it up to the light. "About twenty to five."

"The man the colonel did all this for is supposed to meet his maker at seven. I think we ought to go in there and be witness to it. We couldn't do anything for Maximilian. We can do that much for the colonel."

"You think it's worth the risk?" Brown said. "We've got to think of ourselves, too. We've got to get out of this country some way."

Greenleaf put his hat back on and tugged it into place. "I'm with Slocum. There was a time or two there in the war when the colonel took some risks for me. Seems to me it would be fitting to kind of represent him in there this morning. 'Sides, I'd kind of like to be there. After coming all this way and being so close, wouldn't seem right not to be there."

"I don't agree," Brown said.

"You don't have to," Slocum said. "You and Hodges stay here and fill in the grave. Jim and I'll turn ourselves into priests again. Ought to be plenty priests at an execution. Two more won't be noticed. You keep an eye on those monks and make sure nobody comes nosing around till we get back."

At seven o'clock they were standing in a small crowd on a bare, rocky hill west of the city. A single line of soldiers was holding the crowd back. Beyond the soldiers, facing the firing squad and the crowd and the scattered roofs of Queretaro, were Maximilian and his two generals, Meija and Miramon, their backs to a low adobe wall. Maximilian, dressed in a black suit, wearing a wide white sombrero and looking very tall between his generals, was listening soberly to the words of a priest standing to one side.

Under his breath, Greenleaf said, "Looks like the princess got Juarez to pardon Salm-Salm."

"Likely Maximilian's pleased," Slocum murmured. "Now he can die peaceful."

He watched Maximilian pull a heavy watch out of a vest pocket and snap open the cover. He did indeed look calm and peaceful, considering what he was here for. He had looked that way ever since he'd emerged through the convent's iron gates an hour before.

Slocum and Greenleaf had had the ox cart waiting in a small crowd down the street. They'd gone east and north around the valley this time till they'd found another road into the city. Slocum figured only the main road to Mexico City was being watched, because this one was unguarded, and they'd attracted no attention to themselves on the way in. He'd been surprised at how few people were on the streets and even more surprised that those he saw were dressed in mourning. The troops had been out, though, hundreds of them, crowding the street around three closed carriages in front of the convent's courtyard gates. Slocum had to stand on the cart seat to see when the gates opened and Maximilian and his generals came out, each carrying a crucifix, each accompanied by a priest. Maximilian had towered above everybody else, his thick beard looking very blond in the rising sun. He'd looked calmer than his priest, lifting his head to the sky and breathing deep like a man glad to be up and enjoying the morning air. Then he'd climbed into his carriage, followed by the priest, and the whole procession had started out for this hill.

Up in front of the crowd now, an officer was reading aloud some sort of proclamation. Now he finished and turned back to the firing squad.

"Be over quick now," Greenleaf said.

"Surely ought to be quick," Slocum said. "They got enough firepower."

There were twenty-one men in the firing squad, seven facing each of the condemned men. Now Slocum saw Maximilian go along the line, handing each of his seven men what looked to be a coin. He was pointing at his heart, likely asking for it to be accurate and quick. He'd given his watch to the priest, who looked about to faint. The priest had already come close to fainting once, when they'd descended from the carriages, and it was Maximilian who'd been calmest then, too; the door on his side had stuck, and he'd had to climb out the window, and then the priest had nearly fainted, and Maximilian had brought smelling salts out of his coat to revive the man with. Slocum figured the colonel would have been proud of his Emperor.

Now Maximilian went back to join the generals at the wall. None of them wore anything covering their eyes. He placed the one Slocum figured from the princess's description was Miramon in the honored center position and put Meija on Miramon's right. Then he took the position on Miramon's left and looked to the officer commanding the firing squad.

"Meine Herren, ich stehe Ihnen zu Verfuegung."

The officer approached Maximilian, came to attention, and saluted with his sword. Slocum could tell they were exchanging words, but he was too far away to make them out even if he had been able to speak Spanish. Whatever it was, it seemed to be friendly, or as friendly as it could be under the circumstances. Now the officer saluted again and stepped back to his place by the firing squad.

A hush had fallen over the crowd. In the silence Slocum heard a woman crying. He recognized the woman who had pursued Meija's carriage from the convent, carrying a very young baby, both the baby and the woman shrieking. She'd been hysterical the whole way out of the city and up the hill; once she'd tried to grasp a rear wheel of the carriage and had been thrown to the ground. Miraculously, the baby hadn't been hurt. The troops had marched past her without stopping, and none of the civilians had moved to help, and she had gotten to her feet herself and, still carrying the baby, still crying, had run after the carriage again. Now she had started up again. Slocum figured she had to be Meija's wife, but Meija refused to look at her.

The officer barked out a command, and the seven-man squad in front of Maximilian came to attention. Maximilian himself stood at attention before that adobe wall, without blindfold, without restraints. The crowd was still hushed. The woman continued to cry.

Now Maximilian folded his hands over his heart. *"Viva Mexico!"* he shouted. *"Viva Independencia!"*

Now even Meija's wife fell silent. the officer raised his sword.

"Listos!"

The firing squad brought its rifles up with a flourish.

"Apunten!"

Seven rifles were brought forward and levelled at Maximilian's heart.

"Fuego!"

The sword flashed down. Maximilian seemed to fall backward almost before the sudden rapid, overlapping staccato volley of fire. Black powder smoke rose up above the firing squad, and a loud murmur washed over the crowd. Meija's wife began to shriek again. Slocum could see Maximilian through the smoke, twitching on the ground, his chest a mass of bloody holes. He knew the man had taken too many balls through the heart to be alive, but he was still twitching. When the spirit was strong, the body took a long time to die.

He caught Greenleaf's eye and wanted to say something but nothing he could think of seemed the right thing to say with that man twitching his last up there. The man they had come all this way to save, and hadn't been able to save. Who was dead now—or would be in a second or two. Who would shortly be in that Mexican earth they had just buried the colonel in.

"They're going to give him the coup de grace," Greenleaf whispered.

The officer had brought up one of the soldiers, who was bending over the body and taking careful aim with a pistol. The shot when it came was curiously flat and short, just a pop, with no echo to it at all. The body jerked once, a puff of dust rising up, and then lay still.

Greenleaf was tugging at the collar of his cassock, like maybe it was too tight on him. "Well, he made his decision. He stuck by it. I guess the colonel would be satisfied with that."

"Nobody can deny he died like a man," Slocum said.

The other two died as well, and as quickly. Meija's wife continued to shriek through it all, but just before he was administered the coup de grace someone had the kindness to take her by the arm and lead her away, clutching her baby. Slocum heard her cries slowly recede away down the hill. The priests were clustered around the bodies now. The officer had put away his sword and waved up a detail of white-clad peasants carrying three cheap pine boxes. Now he rapped out several short commands and ran the firing squad into formation and marched them back into place with the other troops.

The single line of soldiers was pushing the crowd back. Reluctantly, the crowd began to edge away, still trying to see through the legs of those priests. Slocum stood his ground till the soldiers got too close, then Greenleaf took him by the arm and tugged at him.

"Time to leave," he whispered. "We're all right long as we don't have to talk. Let one of those soldiers ask us a question and we're in trouble."

"I believe you're right. I don't want to get searched and have them start wondering why I'm wearing a gunbelt under this thing."

They let the slow drift of the crowd pull them back down the hill to where they had left the burro and the ox cart. When they had mounted to the driver's seat, Slocum took the burro's reins, waiting for the rest of the crowd to pass. The troops were standing in formation at the top of the hill. Black powder smoke was still dissipating above their heads. He could see the adobe wall stretching across it and the small cluster of black-clad priests etched against the very center of it, standing over those bodies.

The sun was still not too far above the horizon. The sky was a brilliant blue, the morning air cool and crisp. He couldn't remember ever seeing a better day.

"Better get back to that abbey," Greenleaf said. "Brown and Hodges are likely getting itchy by now."

"Yes," Slocum said, "better get back there and give some thought to getting out of this whole country."

He took one last look at that black knot of priests up at that low adobe wall. Then he flicked the reins and turned the burro in the tightest circle he could and followed the last of the crowd down into the streets of Queretaro.

GREAT WESTERN YARNS FROM ONE OF THE BEST-SELLING WRITERS IN THE FIELD TODAY

JAKE LOGAN

___ 0-872-16935	ROUGHRIDER	$1.95
___ 0-867-21160	SEE TEXAS AND DIE	$1.95
___ 06551-0	LAW COMES TO COLD RAIN	$2.25
___ 867-21216-0	ACROSS THE RIO GRANDE	$2.25
___ 872-16990-1	BLAZING GUNS	$1.95
___ 0-867-21003	BLOODY TRAIL TO TEXAS	$1.95
___ 0-867-21041	THE COMANCHE'S WOMAN	$1.95
___ 0-867-21022	DEAD MAN'S HAND	$1.95
___ 0-867-21006	FIGHTING VENGEANCE	$1.95
___ 872-16939-1	HANGING JUSTICE	$1.95
___ 872-16795-X	HELLFIRE	$1.95
___ 0-867-21102	IRON MUSTANG	$1.95
___ 867-21229-2	MONTANA SHOWDOWN	$2.25
___ 21134-2	THE NECKTIE PARTY	$1.95
___ 0-867-21051	NORTH TO DAKOTA	$1.95
___ 0-872-16979	OUTLAW BLOOD	$1.95
___ 0-867-21159	RIDE FOR REVENGE	$1.95
___ 0-872-16914	RIDE, SLOCUM, RIDE	$1.95
___ 872-16880-8	SLOCUM'S BLOOD	$1.95
___ 06249-X	APACHE SUNRISE	$2.25
___ 06191-4	THE CANYON BUNCH	$2.25
___ 05956-1	SHOTGUNS FROM HELL	$2.25
___ 06132-9	SILVER CITY SHOOTOUT	$2.25
___ 07398-X	SLOCUM AND THE LAW	$2.50
___ 867-21217-9	SLOCUM AND THE MAD MAJOR	$1.95
___ 867-21120-2	SLOCUM AND THE WIDOW KATE	$1.95
___ 06255-4	SLOCUM'S JUSTICE	$2.25
___ 05958-8	SLOCUM'S RAID	$1.95
___ 06481-6	SWAMP FOXES	$2.25

162a

JAKE LOGAN

___	0-872-16823	SLOCUM'S CODE	$1.95
___	0-867-21071	SLOCUM'S DEBT	$1.95
___	0-872-16867	SLOCUM'S FIRE	$1.95
___	0-872-16856	SLOCUM'S FLAG	$1.95
___	0-867-21015	SLOCUM'S GAMBLE	$1.95
___	0-867-21090	SLOCUM'S GOLD	$1.95
___	0-872-16841	SLOCUM'S GRAVE	$1.95
___	0-867-21023	SLOCUM'S HELL	$1.95
___	0-872-16764	SLOCUM'S RAGE	$1.95
___	0-867-21087	SLOCUM'S REVENGE	$1.95
___	0-872-16927	SLOCUM'S RUN	$1.95
___	0-872-16936	SLOCUM'S SLAUGHTER	$1.95
___	0-425-05998-7	SLOCUM'S DRIVE	$2.25
___	0-425-06139-6	THE JACKSON HOLE TROUBLE	$2.25
___	07182-0	SLOCUM AND THE CATTLE QUEEN	$2.75
___	07183-9	SLOCUM'S WOMEN	$2.50
___	06532-4	SLOCUM'S COMMAND	$2.25
___	06413-1	SLOCUM GETS EVEN	$2.50
___	06744-0	SLOCUM AND THE LOST DUTCHMAN MINE	$2.50
___	07018-2	BANDIT GOLD	$2.50
___	06846-3	GUNS OF THE SOUTH PASS	$2.50
___	07046-8	SLOCUM AND THE HATCHET MEN	$2.50
___	07258-4	DALLAS MADAM	$2.50
___	07139-1	SOUTH OF THE BORDER	$2.50

Prices may be slightly higher in Canada.

Available at your local bookstore or return this form to:

BERKLEY
Book Mailing Service
P.O. Box 690, Rockville Centre, NY 11571

Please send me the titles checked above. I enclose _____. Include 75¢ for postage and handling if one book is ordered; 25¢ per book for two or more not to exceed $1.75. California, Illinois, New York and Tennessee residents please add sales tax.

NAME_____

ADDRESS_____

CITY_____ STATE/ZIP_____

(allow six weeks for delivery)

162b